Pieces of Lace

Jamie McGillian

ISBN:
ISBN-13: 978-0615857121

DEDICATION

To Bailey for being Bailey. And to Devan for being Devan.

Chapter One

The Right Boy for Me

"You up?"

"No," he says. His voice is all gruff and I can tell he really is still asleep.

"Come on. You are."

"I am now. What the hell, Lace?" He sounds mad. I love it when he's mad, because he's never really mad at me. He's just pretend mad.

"Meet me at Starbucks. In ten," I whisper into my phone.

"What? No way. I need sleep. I'm so sleep starved. I need my beauty rest, woman!"

"Shut up!" I joke.

"What time is it?"

"Like you don't know." I glance at the clock. "Eight after eight."

"I shouldn't be up for another three hours. Haven't you heard, teens need their sleep? It's Saturday morning. What the hell are you doing up, Crazy Lacey?"

"Forget it. See you around then," I say, and shut my phone. I turn it off so I don't have to hear it when he calls me back to say that he's sorry, and of course he'll meet my sorry ass.

I'll go myself. I'm always in the mood for a decaf vanilla latte. Any time. So what if it's early and I am never usually up at this hour? The early bird catches the worm. I've got two twenties and a ten. That's what two nights of baby-sitting does for a person like me. It allows me the freedom to sip decaf vanilla latte. Ahhh. I can taste the sweet foam already.

As I head out the door, I make bets with myself. He'll probably show.

I want to get lost in thoughts about him, but I can't. Too freaked out. Seriously, dude, what is weirder than waking up to the sound of your mother doing it with some creep she met two weeks ago? I didn't think it was possible. Didn't think she even knew how to do it. I thought all she thought about was getting the bills in on time, or what I should be doing with my life. I mean, I knew she had to have had sex at least once, or I wouldn't be here, right? So she's done the deed at least once almost seventeen years ago. But I didn't think she had it in her at this point. It's a disgusting thought. If I don't stop thinking about it, I may not be able to enjoy the sweet foam.

Think Starbucks and let everything else go away. Starbucks, with the heavy duty coffee smell, and the music, and the serious coffee drinkers sitting at stations with fingers flying across the keyboards of their laptops. It's all good in Starbucks. It's like a mini- vacation. It's like, "Where are you going for the holidays?" "Oh, we'll be in Starbucks!"

Summer's coming, baby. Just a few more weeks and it will be time to hit the beach. It's warm enough for short sleeves and shorts today. Sweet anticipation. Usually, I dread summer. My mom and I just butt heads for two months. But this is the summer of Jack. I am ready for awesome days at the beach. Awesome nights at the beach. It's going to be good.

Jack alert! Jack is in Starbucks looking extra delicious on this fine morning. His hair, brown and gold, all messy and cute. He must have raced here in his little blue Honda to get here before me. How cute is that? How totally cool is that? It's so cool that I might freak out and run the other way. What the hell is Jack doing here, anyway? Now I have to pretend that I am relaxed when, really, I'm not relaxed because I can't handle having a guy thing going on and it's only been a few weeks and I feel like I might jump off a giant cliff. But that's my secret.

Let the rich aroma of the Starbucks coffee beans fill my senses. Jack is standing against the counter just waiting for me. He's all smiles and a dimple on his left cheek, and really, can I just pass out now, he so damned cute. He's got faded jeans on and a gray T shirt. Melt in my mouth adorable. The guy is perfect. So what is he doing with me?

"Jack? You came?" I say in a mocking tone, and he laughs. That's the thing. He laughs at almost everything I say as if it is the funniest thing he's ever heard.

Once I am in the presence of Jack, my breathing quickens. I also lose my senses.

"Oh, I've been here for hours, just hoping you'd show." He bats his thick eyelashes and smiles and shows his dimples and those big white teeth.

I smile with my whole body, as he pulls me to him in one swift move. Plants his lips on mine. It's brief, but it's loaded. I feel my heart bursting through my chest. I think I might have a heart condition because this can't be normal.

6

Jack and Lacey go together like sluts and high heels, lifeguards and whistles, yin and yang, bats and balls, board shorts and surf boards, and milk and cookies. That's what I'm thinking when we reach the front of the line. "Decaf vanilla latte. Skim milk, please," I say to the barista. I take my money out, but Jack shoves it back in my pocket.

Jack orders two cookies for us, and a tall coffee for himself. Regular. He's not afraid of the caffeine. I, according to Becky, am a monkey on steroids when it comes to caffeine. It gets me jumpy and I can't afford to be jumpy when I'm with Jack.

As we walk to the plush red couches with our delicious hot beverages, I'm wondering if I should keep my mouth shut, or tell Jack what has traumatized me this morning. Jack has met my mom a few times and he thinks she's really nice and normal. Why let the cat out of the bag now? I decide to keep quiet about her sexcapades.

Jack wants me to tell him stuff. He says that's what a real relationship is and I want that, too, but this is too dumb to talk about.

I recognize the scent of Jack's soap. It's like a cinnamon-ocean mix and I want to throw my arms around this guy. As we sit, he puts his arm around me and leans into me so that nobody can hear what he says, but me.

All of a sudden, I am one of those girls that I've watched in chick flicks. I am the happy go lucky girl with the beautiful guy. I am the girl everyone wants to be. It's a lot of pressure. I have to pretend that it's no big deal, but how long will I be able to keep the charade?

"You look good," he whispers.

He's got his hands in my hair and he kisses the tip of my nose.

"Thanks," I say. This is a big one for me. When Jack gives me a compliment, I accept it. Why shouldn't I accept it? I don't roll my eyes. I resist saying, "Really?"

Jack really kisses me. I get that nervous, crazy, happy Jack feeling again. The one that can't truly be described in words. I always get it when Jack is around. It's like a feeling of completeness. I know that sounds cheesy. I can't help it.

Jack leans back with his eyes locked on me as if I am the only girl in the world. His eyes are like navy blue marbles.

We've been like this for about three weeks. It's been the longest and the shortest three weeks of my life. On the one hand, I finally have a boy that I am attracted to who is not a jerk. But on the other hand, I finally have a boy who I am attracted to who is not a jerk. It's a double-edged sword. What if Jack finds out that I am really just a can't-think-straight-mess, and not the cool, funny girl he thinks I am? No matter what, I have to keep him thinking that I am cool as a cucumber.

We met right here in Starbucks heaven. I was on my way home from school when I decided to mosey on in. Jack was at the next table studying for an exam. He is an eleventh grader at the Tollhouse School. I am a tenth grader at Vernon High School. The fact that he is from another school is perfect. If I had to keep up this pretense at school, I could never do it.

I was sitting at a small table next to him, and within seconds he had his eyes on me. It was out of a movie. I was rummaging through my backpack in search of my earphones. I felt his eyes on me, and I decided to give him a show. I stood up to search the pockets of my jeans. I knew I looked good in those jeans. I took out all my crumpled pieces of paper with dumb homework reminders written on them. I took out my hair band, a frayed bracelet that I made in seventh grade. I put it all out on the table.

"Lose something?" Jack leaned into me and asked.

I nodded and said, "Earphones."

I guess the first thing that I noticed about him was his skin. It was perfect. It was naturally tan and so soft and smooth looking. I just wanted to reach out and rub my hands against his face and arms. His smile made me want to take a deep breath and sigh. It was so inviting. Like the ocean on a really hot day.

I didn't smile back. I acted like I was on a mission to find something.

Then Jack stood up from his chair. He was wearing a navy blue polo shirt and faded Levis. He was built in the shoulders, but not too broad, and definitely an athlete. He stuck his hand in his pocket and took out a tangle of earphones and held them out to me in the palm of his hand.

"Here. Use mine."

I was speechless.

Again, that smile.

I didn't know what to do. If I took the earphones, we might not get a chance to talk to each other because I would listen to my music and he would go back to his books.

"I'm Jack," he said.

I'm in love.

"Uh, Lacey."

"Your name is Lacey?" he asked.

"I think so," I said.

He laughed. The best laugh. Kind of silly and sexy at the same time. His eyes were locked on mine. It was crazy.

"Is that a real name?"

"I guess."

"Lacey. It's just right for you," he said.

"Thank you," I laughed.

We stared at each other, but it did not feel awkward.

"Are you studying?" I asked.

"Kind of, but now I am studying you."

It's hot in here.

"So you come here a lot?" I asked.

"I do. Do you?"

"To tell you the truth, I've never been here before. I mean, I've been to Starbucks, but not this one. I am not much of a coffee drinker, but today, I decided to have my first real coffee from Starbucks." I'm babbling, which is never good.

We both laugh.

"So what did you get?"

"Decaf vanilla latte. My friend, Becky recommended it."

"Do you like it?"

"Yum, full bodied flavor," I said.

"Really? How is the aroma?"

"Perfect."

The next thing I knew, we were at the same table chatting away. After like two hours, I really had to go. I didn't want to say goodbye. I was hoping that he would ask for my number or something. I packed up all my stuff and took my time, but he just watched me. I said it was nice talking to him, and he nodded. I had no other choice, but to walk out the door. So I did. I was so pissed that he didn't ask me my number. Damn, I thought, maybe that hadn't gone the way I thought. Just as I started walking toward my house, I heard him call out my name. I smiled and turned around. There he was. Jack asked me if I wanted to hang out the next night and that was it. We had been together ever since.

"So, Jack, what were you doing when I called?" I say in that funny voice I reserve just for him.

Again, he just laughs and pulls me closer to him, my bare legs slung across his lap. It's a good thing I remembered to shave, I think to myself.

"Did you do your math homework?" he asks.

"Yep." I say wrinkling my nose up. Math and I never really liked each other.

"Sweet. Want me to go over it? I love math."

That's another thing about Jack. He is really, really smart. And not in the glasses, suspenders, chess club kind of way. Jack is the guy girls wish they were dating. And he is dating me? "That is so sweet of you, Jack, but no way do I want to waste your time on numbers."

"Think your mom will let you out of the house later?" he says with a mischievous smile decorating his beautiful face.

There I go again. Feeling like I'm on fire.

"I'm sure she will."

"How's your coffee?" he says.

"Like Christmas in a paper cup." I say.

He smiles and rolls his eyes. "Did you really just start drinking this stuff?"

"Yep. You were my first cup." I look at Jack in my most seductive pose, and I am batting my eyelashes.

"You do have that newbie grin when you sip it," Jack says.

We both laugh, and I kiss his cheek, as he twists my wavy dark hair between his fingers. Jack is the best boyfriend in the world.

I could stay like this for hours. So when a text message comes in from my mom, I snap back into reality with a cold jolt.

Mom: Did you forget?

Forget what? What did I agree to do today? Oh no. I forgot about Gramps.

"It's Gramps day," I say to Jack.

"Huh?"

"I forgot about Gramps. We have to go over and see how he is making out today. Things are getting harder for him. He has trouble remembering things," I explain.

"Bummer. This is the Gramps you talk about a lot, right?" he asks.

Of course he remembers that I love Gramps more than anyone else in the world.

"Yep."

"Aren't you going to answer her text?" asks Jack innocently.

"I guess I have to. But I just don't feel like dealing with her."

I feel myself turning into a child. I think Jack can see this transformation. My body shrinks and my voice gets a babyish tone to it.

"Well, you may have to get over that for now if you have to see Gramps today."

He's right, of course.

So I text her back.

Me: Gramps?

Mom: Yep. We have to leave here at noon. Btw, where are u?

She has no idea that I know what ghastly thing she is guilty of.

Me: Starbucks

Mom: With Jack?

Me: Yes

Mom: OK. C u in a little while.

Jack is so cute when he doesn't know what is going on with me. He is looking at me and feeding me little pieces of cookie. As he drops cookie morsels into my mouth, my lips want to reach out and kiss his fingers.

"Jack, you're so sweet."

"Tell me what's up with you and your Mom."

I shake my head no. I can feel myself almost having a tantrum. I must resist turning into a seven year old.

"I know it's only been a few weeks, but I feel close to you, Lace. If something was up in my house, I'd tell you."

That's what he says. Is he the sweetest, or what? How can I let him down?

"Maybe later.

"OK. No biggie. Do we have time to drive to the beach before you have to go?"

"Yes!"

Do we have time? Are you kidding? If I was on my way to the Country Music Awards to accept an award, I'd still make time to go to the beach with Jack.

Since it's only a little after nine, I've got about two hours to hang out and suck face with Jack.

When we get to the beach, it's amazing because there is not a single person there. Jack keeps a blue blanket in his trunk and he spreads it out on the sand. We sit and face the ocean. The water looks so inviting. There is a gentle breeze in the air. The sand is soft and powdery and I like to run my fingers through it.

"Waves look awesome," he says.

"I love the water."

"You do?" he asks.

"I do. I can't wait to swim with you when it's warm," I say.

"That will be awesome," Jack says. And it will.

 Swimming feels so good. If I had to have a sport, it would be swimming. We sit for a few minutes with our hands wrapped around each other just taking it all in. I wish it could always be like this. Right now, I feel so relaxed.

Jack moves in and whispers something in my ear. It startles me.

"What?" I ask, like a loud idiot.

Jack just laughs.

I make a quick recovery. "Boy, what are you whispering for?"

"I want you," he says.

"Well, why didn't you say something?"

The next thing I know, Jack is on top of me. We are kissing. It feels so good. Jack has this technique where his tongue is gentle and warm. Then a pressure builds, and it's not so gentle. Then he throws in this thing where he looks deep into my eyes and pauses before jumping back in to the kiss.

I've kissed three other guys, and let me tell you, none of them can kiss like Jack. Billy Rodriquez kissed all right, but he had sour breath, and I hated his guts. Not a good combo. Petey Malone didn't do anything with his tongue. He just let it hang in my mouth like a big old whale. Like he was renting space in my mouth, but he wasn't paying. Corey Hunter wasn't bad, I guess. It's just that there were no sparks. It was just mechanical kissing, and nothing more. This is so much more.

Time flies when you're making out with Jack on the beach. If I had been in math class, we would just be on the second or third problem. Before I know it, Jack and I have been rolling around in the sand for almost two hours. He's half smile, half serious as he looks in my eyes and makes me want to scream. Jack is the one to remind me that we really should be getting me home so I can see Gramps.

When Jack drops me at the house, I have sand in my pants, sand in my hair, and sand in my fingernails. But I don't care. Jack tells me he is going to be working at Slices, his family's deli this afternoon, but that he will come by and get me tonight at around eight.

"Good luck with Gramps," he waves.

"Thanks, Jack." I get out of the car.

"Have you told him about me yet?" Jack says, in just the cutest little boy tone.

"Told him what?" I act like I have no idea what he's saying.

"Well, if he is so special to you, I'd think you'd tell him about me." His hair is tousled from rolling in the sand.

"I did, Jack. I told him over the phone a week ago. I'm not sure if he'll remember."

"Oh," Jack nods and tries not to look hurt. "What did you say?"

"I told him I met this really strange guy," I joke.

"Lacey!" he says.

"Gotta go, Jack-o-lantern. See you later."

I am back in reality. Back to the house with the mom who just had sex.

My mother, the cuddly first grade teacher, who hasn't gone on a date in my lifetime. Urgh. Now I have to face her and there's no way I want her knowing what I know about her.

Chapter Two

Seeing Gramps

"Hey," I say.

"Hey yourself."

Mom is smiling ear to ear. Dressed in her black pants and red blouse, she looks more like a teller at a bank, than a first-grade teacher.

"Only three more weeks of school. Yes!" she exclaims. "Did you eat?" she asks, while she studies the school calendar.

I don't respond verbally. I do walk to the table and stick a bunch of red grapes in my mouth. The juice oozes out all over my face.

"Pretty!" says Mom.

I chuckle.

"Napkin?" asks mom, handing me one.

"Thanks."

Mom puts down the calendar to look at me. Her full attention. Crap.

"Well, you look happy, Lacey Face."

Urgh.

Mom looks down at the table. Then she looks up at me.

"I've got a bad feeling about Gramps. When I talked to him yesterday, he sounded so confused. I don't think he knew it was me."

Mom talks to me like I'm her therapist. I can't stand it. That's not my job.

"Let's go. The sooner we get there, the sooner we can deal with it. Let me just hit the bathroom," I say. I have got to get some of the sand out of my pants.

"Lacey, what would I do without you?" Mom is saying as we get into her SUV.

I ignore her. I hate when she tries to build me up like that. She is always saying I'm so mature, but the thing is, that is total bullshit. I'm not mature at all. I'm as immature as I can be.

"You always want to deal with the problem. That's an excellent quality," says Mom.

Right. Whatever you say. Who knows where you would be without me? Just watch the road.

"It's not that I want to deal with a problem, but I know it's better to face it head on," I offer.

"Well, it's very proactive and grown-up of you!" Mom says.

Urgh.

The ride is about 15 minutes. I turn up the radio and belt out a few tunes and Mom actually joins me. We park the car and Mom carries a bag filled with things that Gramps likes to eat: licorice, fresh string beans, cheese-filled Danish, and Cheese its. All his favorites.

"Crap," Mom says.

"Crap," I agree.

Gramps lives in a tiny shack that he calls paradise. The front door is open, but the screen door is closed.

"Gramps!" I shout. "Hey Big Guy?"

Mom reaches for the door and opens it.

The TV is blasting a game show. Gramps is sprawled on the couch in nothing but some whitey tighties. Only, they don't look so white. He's definitely alive because he's snoring loudly. The place smells like something died and then came back to life. Gross.

"Dad, Dad?" Mom calls out, panic pouring out of her pores.

I don't want to see Gramps in his undies. I turn away and look at the place. It's a major disaster. There's pieces of mail everywhere. His kitchen table is a mass of papers and pennies. He's got thousands of pennies covering every surface. In the kitchen, dirty dishes are piled up. Food is out on the counters and there's a certain smell that makes me gag. I've got to do something, besides run out of the place, so I begin to wash the dishes. I find a sponge and some dish soap and I start to clean, clean, clean. I can hear Mom in the background. Her voice is strained. It sounds like Gramps has finally gotten up. His voice is all scratchy.

"What are you doing?" Gramp calls out to Mom.

"What do you mean, we have a date. Lacey's here. Lacey?" she calls to me, desperation in her voice.

"Lacey?" Gramps doesn't sound like he knows who I am.

"Gramps," I rush out to the living room. "You're up! Late night last night? Hot date?" I'm nervous so I'm making my dumb jokes and moving around the room.

Mom has covered him up a bit. Thank God. He's got a blanket hiding his man stuff.

Gramps is looking at me like he can't quite get a handle on who I am.

"Rosey?" he asks. "Rosey!"

Gramps has a confused look on his face.

"No, Gramps. It's me. Lacey.   Your favorite granddaughter. Your only granddaughter."

Rosey was my grandmother. She died about five years ago. Hmmmm. I guess he thinks I am his wife.   That's creepy, but so sad. But Rosey was a really beautiful woman so I feel honored.

Gramps is still bugging out a bit. Not quite sure what to think about me, and also, a little annoyed that his daughter has come to wake him out of a thick sleep.

"Can you get cleaned up? Lacey and I are going to take you to lunch. How does that sound, Dad?" my mom says, making a transition to her gentle first-grade-teacher voice.

"Lunch?" Gramps says.

"Today?" he asks. "I am hungry."

His eyes are watery and blood shot. He smiles.

Mom nods her head, and I smile and go back to the kitchen sink, where I have managed to let the water run, and boy, did I make a mess on top of a mess.

I concentrate on cleaning the kitchen as my mom takes her dad into his bedroom to get dressed. I feel bad that she has to do that. I know it must be hard. I try not to think about it, just as I try not to think about Mom getting some. My thoughts are interrupted with Mom's moaning from hours ago, and an occasional image of Gramps naked, and it's all just too much for a young girl to bear. But when I try to think about my hot boyfriend, I go weak at the knees. So I just think about the task at hand.   Cleaning the dishes. Drying the dishes. Putting away the dishes.

Throwing out the food on the counters. Sponging the counters. Taking out the garbage. Putting away the stuff Mom brought Gramps. In about 20 minutes, I have accomplished the task. I am rather proud of myself, as I take it all in. The kitchen is clean, although I still smell that funky smell.

Mom is helping Gramps with his belt. He's gotten so skinny. But this time, when I walk in the living room, he sees me and knows me. With a big grin he says, "How's my girl?" I smile and turn into a five-year-old. Gramps has such charm. My mom said he could make any woman smile.

"I'm good, Gramps. Good to see you."

"Get over here, Lace. Give your Gramps a hug."

And I do. And then he's talking to me and remembering things. He is asking about math. Urgh. Everyone asks me about math. He even remembers that I have a boy named Jack in my life. He asks how things are going with my gentleman caller. Gentleman caller! So Gramps. His voice is loud and scruffy.

In the car, it takes a while to get Gramps settled in the front seat. He argues that he doesn't want the seatbelt on him, and then Mom gets so upset she says that she can't drive without him being belted. He sneers at her. I get out of the car and put the belt on him and give him a kiss on the cheek and he seems ok with that. He gives me a smile and a wink.

"By the way, I don't like cheese Danish anymore. Don't buy it for me, you hear that?"

Mom nods and looks away.

She takes everything he says so personally. He's only trying to press her buttons. He's just playing.

It's a beautiful day. I've got Jack all over me and as I think about him, I get all hot and bothered.

At the diner, Gramps complains about the prices. He says he can't believe that these days you can't get a sandwich for less than ten bucks. He says its highway robbery. I laugh, but Mom gets really annoyed with him. When the waitress comes to the table, Gramps starts to lecture her about the meaning of good service. The waitress tries to be respectful, but finally she ignores Gramps, turns to my mom, and asks what he's having. Mom is acting like Gramps is being a very naughty boy. But Gramps is just being Gramps. He's just trying to make sure that people are listening to him.

I get a cup of creamy tomato soup and a turkey sandwich. All that making out this morning has given me a raging appetite. I smile to myself. Mom orders a chef salad with the dressing on the side. Very good choice. I wink at her. If it weren't for her little secret love affair, she might be ordering fries and a grilled cheese. Gramps has a burger. He always has a burger. He says, 'they can't ruin a burger.' He says he would like his burger with "French fried potatoes." The waitress nods and says, "French fries" and Gramps says, "No, French-fried potatoes." OK then. Gramps is causing a bit of a scene. I explain that French fries are the same thing as French fried potatoes. He looks at me like I'm crazy. He shakes his head.

I am too full to eat everything on my plate, so Gramps starts giving me a lecture about not wasting. Waste not, want not is his motto. I tell him he's right, and, that I promise next time I will clean my plate.

I can see that my mom is worried about my Grandfather. When she says she's going to the restroom, I wonder if it's because she's upset.

"How are those French-fried potatoes?" I ask.

Gramps sticks a fork into a big piece of potato and holds it out to me to taste. I bite into it and tell him it's yummy.

I tell Gramps that I will be right back, I'm just going to check on Mom. He gives me a great big smile, as he bites into another French-fried potato.

I find my mom in the bathroom hunched over by the sink.

"Mom?" I say.

"That man," she says. "He's going to drive me nuts. I don't know what to do with him." Mom is applying lipstick like a mad woman.

"It will work itself out," I say. "He's just being Gramps."

"He's nice to you, but he doesn't like me," she says.

"That's crazy. He loves you."

"Easy for you to say," she barks.

Later, we deposit Gramps back to his house and tell him that we will be back next Saturday for a special visit. We usually see him twice a month, but waiting that long to see him again just doesn't feel right. I put my arms around him and tell him I adore him.

"It's you I love the most, Lacey," he says. My heart just melts. Gramps has turned into a child.

Before we leave, Gramps asks Mom to bring black and white cookies with her next time. He tells her he never liked cheese Danish and that she should not bring them ever again. Mom stares at him. On the way home, Mom is talking about her father. She says he never showed his love. She said it was always difficult for her to talk to him. Blah, blah, blah. I, however, have tuned out. I am having a Jack attack.

This is a Jack attack: You are in the middle of living your life. Maybe you are watching Big Bang Theory repeats. Maybe you are cutting up some veggies for a salad. Maybe you are putting on your favorite sweat pants. All of a sudden, you get this flutter, this chill up your spine. You hear the word, Jack. All your senses become numb. You can't believe that this world, which contains such beautiful things as sapphires and coffee beans and beaches and rivers and chocolate and lilacs and puppies, also contains Jack. Jack. He's this crazy mad boy who is really into you and he's got dimples and he makes you smile a smile that just wants to leap out and grab Jack. That's a Jack attack. You should know that you should not be operating heavy or large machinery during a Jack attack. You don't want to be behind the wheel or in the middle of hammering a nail. When the Jack attack passes, you just want to be very still and let it drift over you until you return to the planet.

I'm thinking about what to wear tonight. I'm wondering if I should straighten my hair. Jack hasn't seen me with straight hair yet. It could be a major turn on. I'm also thinking about wearing a short dress with boots. And perfume. And body lotion. I'm also thinking about going all the way.

Chapter Three

My One and Only

Katy Perry is blasting in the bathroom, as I am straightening my hair. Becky is sitting on the toilet seat cover watching the transformation of Lacey Ann Bryce. Mom has let me know that she is going out with a friend. I am careful not to ask her any questions. I just nod. She says she'll be home by midnight. I say I will be home by midnight, as well. She leans forward to kiss me on the cheek, but I pull away.

"Whoa, Mom, I could have burned you."

"I just wanted a little kissy," she says, looking wounded.

"Yeah, but a flat iron is a dangerous weapon."

I tell her she looks nice. She does, actually. She's wearing a blue dress and her dark hair is in a neat ponytail. She's got on eyeliner and just a little purple eye shadow.

"Have fun," I say.

"You too. Where are you going?"

"Not sure. Maybe a movie or something."

"Well, you look lovely."

Becky tells Mom that she looks hot and then she gives her a kiss. Mom loves Becky. Becky loves Mom. They make small talk for a while. I am thinking Jack thoughts.

I didn't exactly tell Jack that I was going to go all the way tonight, so I could back out at any time. But tonight I just feel crazy. I am tired of being a virgin, and I just want to get it over with. I know that if I told Becky that, she would freak out on me. She would tell me that I should not do it just to get it over with, just to change my status. But that's not really the way I feel. I want to do it with Jack. I'm ready to do it with Jack. He's the one.

Becky is not a virgin and she is always saying that she regrets going all the way with Neil Hoffman and Tom Ditz. Hoffman was her first and he treated her like gold until he popped her cherry. A few days later, he broke up with her. Only he didn't even have the balls to do it in person. He had his friend pass her a note in chemistry class. The note read: I think we've outgrown each other. Let's see other people. Yours truly, Hoff. She was devastated. She didn't go out again for weeks. Then there was Tom. Tom is a great person. I used to be friends with him and his sister, Kiki in grade school. Tom is cute and athletic, but he's on the sensitive side. He hangs out with a lot of girls, and he is very brainy. Tom loved Becky so much. He admired her from afar. Every day, he would just stare at her and smile. Finally, one day, as we were eating our grilled cheese sandwiches in the cafeteria, she said, "Oh, what the fuck!" And I said, "Excuse me?" and she said "Tom. What the hell is he staring at?" And I said, "You. He loves you." And then she got up and walked over to him. He couldn't believe it. I couldn't believe it. It was so unBecky. Becky is really pretty and she has huge boobs. She sat right down next to him and gave him one of her big winning smiles. That's it. The guy was hooked. For a few days, Becky managed to rock Tom's world. And Becky looked fairly happy. She walked down the halls holding hands with Tom and waiting for any sign of Hoffman. But if Hoffman did see, he never let on that he cared. He had moved on and was dating at least half of the cheerleading squad.

I really thought that Becky and Tom made a great match, and not just because Tom Sawyer's girlfriend was named Becky. Tom was smart enough for Becky's wit and he let her be her edgy self. Becky gave Tom a run for the money. She gave him a makeover, and turned him into a hot guy. When I asked her how she did it, she told me she plucked his eyebrows, bought him some Axe, took him shopping, and told him to get contact lenses. After a few weeks of going out, they did it. Tom was so in love with her, he practically wanted to marry her, but Becky freaked out. She told him she needed her space and that she wanted to have sex with other people. Just like Hoff had done to her. She pulled the plug on that relationship. Now she's with some skanky guy named Keith, who she met at the boardwalk. Jack knows Keith and says he's a sleaze ball. Becky slept with him the night she met him. She said she doesn't give a crap about it anymore. She says Hoffman deflowered her and ruined her. Every time I think about Becky, it makes me sad. She is beautiful and smart and tough. Hoffman is an ass. I can't look at him.

"Becky, do I look too over the top?" I ask.

"Absolutely," she says. "Now can you get out of your bathroom, I have to go. Mexican food. Bad things happening. Hurry!"

I run out of the bathroom, before Becky gets too detailed. She is always talking about bodily functions. It's totally gross. She is so open, it's crazy. I'm always saying, "Beck, too much information!" But she just doesn't get it.

I think about how Jack is different from all other guys. I can be myself around him. Well, almost. Or, at least, the self that I like to project. The best thing about being with Jack is that he doesn't go to my school. I don't have to worry about what I wear every day. I don't have to spy on him, or have that butterfly feeling every time I catch a glimpse of him.

I think I look pretty by the time I have finished preparing myself for the night. My hair is long, silky, and straight. It's a lot longer than I ever imagined. Right down to my elbows. I'm wearing my favorite cowboy boots and a swishy sea foam colored mini dress. I've got smoky eyes and lots of eyeliner on. I can hardly recognize myself in the mirror.

"Holy Shit!" Becky says.

"What?"

"You look totally hot. Like a rock star. Just look at you. My little Lacey is really growing up! It's sick! It brings tears to my eyes," Becky goes on.

"Do you need to ask me any questions? You are definitely losing it tonight. Nobody would be able to keep their hands off you. You look sizzling, smoking. What a babe!"

"Get out of here, now!" I say. We both get hysterical.

Becky gives me a hug and a kiss and then she leaves. She's off to a movie with one of her gay guy friends. Becky has a lot of gay guy friends.

For a moment, I'm wondering if I should just put my jeans on and just play it safe. Play it safe. Do I want to play it safe? I am just about to go for the jeans when I get a text from Jack saying that he is outside. I think about inviting him in, but I just can't handle that. I mean, he has been inside my house before. He even came over one night to watch a movie, but Mom was home. Do I ask him to come in when I know my mom is out for a while? I don't trust myself.

When I open the front door and walk out on the porch, Jack is standing there. He is wearing faded jeans, a brown polo shirt, and boat shoes. Damn, he looks cute. He is staring at me with a wide grin.

"Whoa, look at you, Lacey girl?"

"What do you mean?"

"You look amazing. Look at your hair. And how about those legs? I think I've died and gone to heaven. You look like a model, girl."

My face feels hot. I know I must be blushing big time.

"Come here," Jack says.

I walk toward him and stop an inch before he starts. I can smell him. The ocean. The sweet cinnamon. And something else. Peppermint gum. He's got such an aura about him.

He gives me the sweetest, most innocent kiss.

"Change of plans. I have to think for a minute."

He runs his hands through his hair and paces on the porch.

"What's up?" I ask.

"Well, we were going to go to Moe's. But under the circumstances, I don't think I want to go there. I want to take you some place special. Let me think."

He takes out his phone and calls someone.

"Hey Ma," he says. I just want to gobble up this guy.

"Yea. What's the place Pop took you for your anniversary?"

He is nodding.

"Yes, that's the one. Yes. I know where it is. Thanks, Mom. Have a good night. You too. I will."

"I got an idea." His eyes are lit up and for the first time, I can almost make out what he must have been like as a child, all wide-eyed and angelic. This guy does it for me.

I smile.

He takes a picture of me on his phone. Then he stands next to me, holds the phone up and takes a picture of us. "That's for Facebook."

How cute is that?

"My mom said to tell you hello," he says almost shyly.

"Oh, that was so sweet of her," I gush.

Jack's mom is pretty and smart. She runs Slices, the deli, and a catering business. Jack's dad works in computers. They live two towns away in a really nice Tudor house.

"Let's go," he says, and he grabs my hand.

Jack takes me to a fancy restaurant overlooking the water. It's called Blue. It's dark and romantic inside and we are seated by a window that faces the harbor. Jack acts like an adult in the restaurant. He knows how to talk to people and get what he wants. He orders the shrimp and rice and I have grilled chicken and mashed potatoes. It's the best dinner I have ever had in my life. I eat most of my meal, but when Jack asks if I want dessert, I tell him that he's sweet enough for me. He rolls his eyes and grins. Being at the restaurant with Jack is really great, but I want to be alone with him. I think Jack feels the same way because he is all about getting a check suddenly.

As we walk to the car, I thank him for dinner. He puts his arm around me and kisses me. When we are in the car, he rests his hand on my thigh.

"Do you want to get high? I got some killer weed," he says.

As much as I wouldn't mind taking a few hits to relax, I am scared of getting high and acting like a jerk. I've done pot a few times with Becky, but I'm really not sure it had much of an effect on me. But I'm not a party pooper.

"Yeah, sure. Sounds good. We've never done this together yet. It's a first," I comment.

Jack nods. "I love our firsts."

He stretches across the seat and gives me a wicked kiss. I can't wait to get to the beach. He drives to the beach and then we stay in the car while he lights a joint. He takes a hit and passes it off to me. I take it, as if I've taken a hundred joints.

"I don't do this often," he explains. "You can't when you play sports, but I got this from a buddy and it's really good stuff. Trust me. We are going to have fun."

I nod and take a hit like I am a champion smoker.

"Whoa there," Jack says. "The joint almost went down your throat you took it so hard." Jack is laughing.

I giggle as I hold in the smoke. I have just sucked in ashes. Yum. I start to cough. I'm such a jerk.

Music plays softly and I think it's John Mayer. I can hardly contain my feelings for Jack. I just want to get out of the car and find a spot on the beach and jump his bones. But Jack is taking it slow, and he seems to want to talk. It must be the effect of the pot. I take another toke of the weed, but this time I do it slower because Jack is watching me.

I begin to feel really free. That's the only word I can think of. I can't think of any place I'd rather be. I am the luckiest girl in the whole state of New York to have this beautiful guy like me. I run my fingers through my hair and it feels foreign to me. I'm not used to having such fine hair. Jack is watching me. The clock on the dashboard reads 9:38. I've got the whole night ahead of me with this guy. Life is perfect. I just want to bottle this feeling forever. But then, I get paranoid.

I can't say for sure, but I think there might be someone out there.

"Is someone watching us?" I ask Jack.

The car is definitely filled with smoke, so it's not easy to see. Jack is parked in a deserted spot, but on a Saturday night, there is always some traffic. Jack looks out and tells me we are good, but I just can't let it go. I feel like there is a shadowy figure in the distance.

"I think we are being watched, Jack."

Suddenly, it's like an alarm that goes off in my whole body. Instead of being able to focus on Jack and his divine self, I am freaking out that there is someone watching us.

"Babe," he says. "It's just your imagination."

Babe. That is the first time that he has called me that. Call me an ambulance.

I want this guy so much, but I have to get the evil thoughts out of my head. I start thinking this could be the plot of a teenage horror flick. It's perfect. Weird girl wants awesome guy. She's over the top for the guy. She would do anything, be anything for the guy. Girl and guy hook up, and the love songs play. But then a guy with an axe opens the door.

"Are the doors locked?" I ask. I am now shriveled up against the car door.

"Lace, listen to me. You are fine. Just a little paranoid from the weed. It's perfectly normal. Come here, babe."

That's it. Somebody call 911.

"But I can't stop thinking that there is someone outside watching us. What if there is?"

"Shhhh. I promise we are safe."

I want to believe him, but I can't shake the feeling that there is someone out there.

"Would you feel better if I go outside and walk around?" he asks

"No!" I shout, just like a lunatic. "Are you crazy? They will kill you."

Why did I smoke weed? That is not something good for someone like me.

"Come here. Let me make you feel safe," Jack says, he's smiling and I can tell he thinks I am an absolute moron.

Oh. I really, really want to. I want to be close to Jack. Jack is where I want to be. I lean toward him, but just as I do, I am certain that I see someone standing in front of the car. A figure or a shadow.

"There's someone out there," I gasp.

Jack steps out of the car. In an instant, he is on my side of the car opening the door.

"Come on outside, Lace. Let's get some air. There's no one around. And if there are people, they're not looking at us."

I go slowly. I am still afraid, but I go. Jack is right. There is nobody outside by the car. There are some people in the distance, but I must have been hallucinating. I start to feel like a moron.

"I'm sorry, Jack. I don't know what happened. Usually, I'm so cool when I smoke weed."

Jack laughs. He knows I'm a jerk.

"No worries. Come on, let's get the blanket out of the trunk and hit the beach. Do you still want to?" he asks.

I nod.

I'm glad to be out of the car. Sitting in the car was making me feel claustrophobic. Once I am outside, I feel a lot better. I take Jack's hand as he grabs the blanket and we head toward the beach.

"What a night. Look at all those stars, Lacey Face," says Jack, pointing to the sky.

It's a stellar night. And, I'm ready for it to get even better. I am prepared to rock Jack's world. There's only one thing standing in my way. I have to pee. I try to block the thought out of my head. I can hold it. I can hold it. I tell myself. But, as we hit the sand, I start to wonder if I really can hold it. The sensation that I have to pee is getting worse with every step I take. I am in a panic.

Oh, the agony of having to pee. I curse the two sodas I had in the restaurant. And listening to the sound of the ocean doesn't help matters. I will never be able to last.

"Jack," I blurt out in a panic. I stop walking and look at him.

"What's wrong, Babe?" he asks.

Oh God.

"I really, really, really have to pee," I say. I am miserable. I am ruining the night.

Jack slowly smiles at me, and shakes his head in wonder.

"It's OK. Walk over to the dunes. I'll wait right here for you. Peeing won't be hard because you're not wearing pants. It's OK, Lacey. Do you want me to come with you? I promise I won't look, unless you want me to." Jack winks at me.

"No, don't really need you seeing me pee. But, thanks for the offer."

"Any time!" Jack says.

I nod. I am going to be all right. I get excited when I realize that I have tissues in my dress pocket so I don't have to drip dry. I take off my boots and leave them with Jack. Then I hurry toward the dunes. I don't want him to see me, so I figure I will wait until he is out of sight, before I drop my drawers. The only thing I can think about right now is peeing. I can't wait to empty my bladder. I find a spot that seems really out of the way. I don't see anyone. I don't hear anything. I am good to go. I hunch down and take off my lacey panties. Then I squat down in the sand and get ready to do my business. All of a sudden, I am frozen. I can't pee. I still have to pee, only I can't do it. Shit, this sucks.

Get a hold of yourself Lacey Jane, I tell myself. You are not the first girl to pee on the beach with a hot guy in the distance. Pee or else. I start to pinch myself to punish myself for causing me such grief. Why are you doing this to me? I say to myself. My fingers squeeze the flesh on my left forearm. Damn it. Breathe. I just need to relax and breathe. OK. Pee. Nothing. Pee. Nothing. That's when I start to cry. Stupid baby. Do not cry. Do you know what your eyes will look like if you cry? You will be a mess. You are fine. You are fine. This is nothing. In the real world, this isn't even a challenge. You are just going to let yourself relax. That's it. I roll my head around in a very slow circle. This helps me. I begin to feel relaxed. I can do this. I can do this. I can pee. That's right. I squat. I wait. I pray. Come on. Think of water and wet things. Let's go. Who is doing this to me? Finally, a tiny trickle. But then, golden happiness shoots out of me in a thick stream. Ahhhhhh. It feels so good. It seems to go on for hours. Ahhhhhh. Yes. I am good. I have peed. I have wiped. I have put back my panties. I am so good to go back to Jack, to the love of my life. Only problem is, I can't seem to remember which direction I need to go in. Shit.It's so dark. I stand still and look for clues to tell me which way I need to go. I don't remember any details. Everything looks the same. I can feel those stupid tears again. I decide to go 10 steps in every direction. I will stop and look to see if I can find Jack after I take 10 steps. This is crazy. Where's Jack?

"Jack?" I call out. I don't see him anywhere.

Why me? I've lost Jack. This can't be happening.

Suddenly, I see something in the distance. It's a figure coming toward me. At first, I think it might be an axe murderer. I am playing right into his plan. He will kill me, for sure. This is nuts. What am I doing here?

"Lacey?"

"Whose there?" I ask.

"Lace?"

"Jack? Is it you?" I ask. My voice sounds desperate.

"Who else would it be? You OK?"

"Oh, yeah! I mean, now I am. I just got lost for a second, but I'm good to go now." I am rambling now. "I couldn't pee, Jack. It was terrible. Such an awful feeling. You have to go, but you can't."

"Did you go?"

"Yes!"

Jack has wrapped his arms around me now. "That's a good girl," says Jack. "Race you to the blanket," he says.

I run like lightning, but he's still faster than me. He's waiting for me. He leads me to the soft fuzzy baby blue blanket that he has laid out. I love this blanket. It's the love blanket.

We both sit and then lie on our backs and look at the stars for a while. Suddenly, I feel shy.

Jack is driving me crazy. He is looking deep into my eyes and smiling slightly. He is not touching me. At all. I don't know what to do with myself. I feel like a child and Jack is an adult. That's pretty dumb, considering that he is only a year older than me. Jack is just gazing at me. God, I am such a jerk. Slowly, he covers his face in my face. His lips are soft as silk. My heart is beating so hard. Jack!

"Jack," I whisper.

"Yeah?"

"Jack, I'm ready."

Jack freezes and looks up at me. He knows what I'm talking about.

"Are you sure?" he asks. "It's not too soon?"

"I'm so ready," I say. I feel like I am trying to convince him.

"Let's talk about this, Lace. I want it, too, believe me, but, we really don't have to rush. We have all the time in the world. It hasn't even been a month."

"But it feels right and I feel ready. I want this."

Oh my God. Am I trying to convince him to have sex with me? What is wrong with me?

"Isn't it the guy's job to want it more than the girl?" I say.

Jack is whispering in my ear. Something about what it feels like when he kisses me. I can't quite make it out. He's kissing my neck and making me feel like I want to scream out the lyrics to my favorite Christmas songs. I have to force myself not to do it. I have to tell myself to be cool. Do not shout out something lame, like "Rocking around the Christmas tree." Thank God I only say this in the safety of my own head.

Jack's hand is riding up my skirt slowly and softly. His touch is like a billion tiny feathers. It's the most incredible feeling. I so want to cry out, but I resist. Resist. Then he stops. He is not touching me. He is looking deep into my eyes and I am petrified.

"Lacey," he says. His voice is so gentle. "Are you sure?"

"What's wrong? Don't you want to, Jack?" I whisper.

"More than you know," he says.

"Well, than, what are you waiting for?" I ask.

"Just making sure that it's you talking and not the pot," he says.

Can you believe that? He's so nice.

I make a funny voice. "This is Lacey Bryce talking, Jack. I want it. Now."

Jack laughs. But then no more laughing and just a tense feeling. I don't know what's going to happen next. I'm scared, but I am ready. Now, I wait to see what Jack's next move will be.

Jack is thinking.

I am waiting.

Jack is moving toward me so slowly.

His kiss builds in such an amazingly hot way. I am breathing so heavily.

"Jack, the way you kiss, it should be illegal," I whisper.

I mean for that to sound sexy. Instead it sounds so stupid that Jack cracks up. He just cracks the hell up. He is sitting up on the blanket and holding his sides and having a big belly laugh. At first, I'm not sure what is so funny. I have trouble remembering what I just said, and then, when those words come to me, "Jack, the way you kiss, it should be illegal." I am laughing so hard now. At first, it is extreme pleasure, but then it actually hurts. It hurts to laugh so hard. I want to stop, but I can't. When I look at Jack, I just can't help but laugh. I don't even know why. It goes on forever. My face hurts from keeping it stuck in laugh position. I need to stop, but it's not even dying down. It's still going on full force. Now I'm scared that I will go on like this forever. I have to think of sad thoughts. Sad things. Sad things. I think of Gramps on the couch when he didn't recognize me. That was sad. And when he thought that I was his wife. That was sad. So why am I hysterically laughing? Oh no. Please God, give me the strength to stop laughing. Jack is just hanging back enjoying the view. His laugh has slowed to a nice pace, but mine has not. Oh, the agony.

"Please, Jack, you have to help me," I plead.

"What's wrong, babe?" he says.

I am still stuck in big smile and laugh mode. "Make me stop laughing!"

So he puts his arms around me and rocks me slowly back and forth. I crush my face into his neck and desperately try to straighten my face muscles. Slowly, the laugh begins to fall away from me. I am relieved to say the least.

Jack has a huge smile on his face.

"You are so funny and adorable. What am I going to do with you?" he asks.

The next thing I know, my bra is unhooked, my dress has been removed and Jack is on top of me. Suddenly I don't feel like laughing. I'm just going with the flow. I'm just crossing over from virgin to non-virgin. And, while I like it, there is something very scary about it.

When we are done, Jack is holding me close.

"You OK?"

I nod. I am OK.

"You happy?" he asks.

I nod.

"I can't wait until next time, Lace."

I nod.

Next time? He actually wants to do this again? That means that I was good. I mean, I know he was good, but I didn't know I was good. That's a relief.

Jack gives me a smile and moves in for the longest kiss in history.

On the way home, we're both quiet. I can still feel Jack's fingers on me. I feel kind of sore down there.

"You tired?" Jack asks.

"I'm hungry. I can eat three sandwiches now."

Jack nods.

"I know that feeling."

"I had a great time, Lacey. You are the best."

Jack kisses my neck. I smile. I have like a pound of sand in my panties and my hair is no longer smooth or straight, but I know I still look good.

Jack asks if I want to stop to get something to eat, but I kind of just want to go home. He tells me that tomorrow he's going to church with his family. He's not sure if he will have time to get together. I brush it off like it's fine with me.

"I promised Becky I'd hang out with her, anyway," I say.

"Are you all right?" he asks.

I nod. I am all right. I just feel older suddenly.

"Good night, Lace."

"Good night, Jack."

He winks. Then he waits for me to walk inside my house. My mom isn't home yet, so I head for the kitchen. I have a serious case of the munchies. As I make myself a small buffet of peanut butter and crackers, black olives, and cold pasta, I keep going over the details of the night. The way Jack looked at me when he saw me at the beginning of the date. The romantic restaurant. Jack's face when I said that someone was outside the car. He was so protective and brave. How about when he called me babe? Could that have been any hotter?

What I don't want to think about is the fact that Jack and I did it. I'm not ready to face that just yet. I still want to think about the little details. His smile. His kiss. His scent.

My phone buzzes. Text message.

Your kisses should be illegal.

Ha! Did I really say that? Jack. I love him.

Chapter Four

I Want Things to Stay the Same

I put on my favorite flannel pajamas, the ones with the penguins marching on the pink background. I shut the light, climb into bed and think for just a minute about everything that's happening. Mom is definitely late because it is a quarter to one already, and she said she would be home by twelve. Mom. What am I going to do with her? Then there's Jack, who is wonderful, but I don't know if I deserve him, and I don't know if I can pull it all off. And now that we've gone this far, what happens? Do we always do it when we see each other? Will he expect it? I thought I would want to tell Becky the second I did it, but I don't feel like talking about it. I just want it to be our secret. What if now that I have given myself to Jack, there is no excitement for him? What if he is bored with me? What if I become bored with him? Now that I am not a virgin, will I want to sleep with every boy I am attracted to? What happens when I go away to college? Will I take birth control with me just because I'm a sexually active girl? There's too much to think about. I just want to go back to the beginning of the night when things weren't so complicated. I reach for Libby, my stuffed duck. Libby, the last thing I got from my dad before he left for Las Vegas. My dad. I can't even make out his face.

I wake up at three in the morning. My head hurts and my tummy feels too full. Urgh. Did I really eat peanut butter and black olives? As I try to wish myself back to sleep, I can't believe what I hear next. It's Mom and she is not alone. Mom is having sex again. I am repulsed. Why is this happening to me? Why can't things just stop, and go back to the way they were? Why does Mom need to have sex? Why did I need to have sex? Why did I meet Jack? Why did Mom meet this sex-starved loser? What's going to happen to us? Will I have to meet this guy and be civil to him? Will he like me, or will he see me as an obstacle? Am I the teenage child who tries to get in his way? Maybe he is a nice guy. Why should I think that he is a loser, just because he is in bed with my mother? My mother is not a loser. She's great, actually. She's pretty and bright. Kids love her. She's the favorite first grade teacher at the Krauss School, where she teaches. She's funny. She likes to read aloud to children using like a dozen different voices. The kids really get a kick out of it. I know I did when I was younger. I'd be like, "Can you read it again, Mom, just one more time?" And she always did. It might have been Where the Wild Things Are, or, Are You My Mother? But we also loved Dr. Seuss. And sometimes, Mom just made up stories with ridiculous characters. Some were spooky and mean and others were sweet and dumb. Sometimes we'd act out the stories together. I loved that. Good times.

I hold Libby tight. I must still be high because I go to sleep thinking about how great my mom is and how lucky I have been to have her in my life.

In the morning, I forget all about my incredible mother, who happens to be sleeping late. I decide the best thing to do is to head straight to Starbucks for a coffee, this time with caffeine. I need to be super alert today. I've got a lot of thinking to do. I'm quiet as I walk out of the house. It's a beautiful day. Such a tease. I would believe it was almost summer from the warm, gentle breeze. As I walk, I suddenly remember that Jack said he would be going to church today. Church? I didn't know he was religious. I'm not religious at all. I mean, I don't think I am. I haven't stepped into a church in over a decade. The last time I went anywhere religious, it was to Becky's bat mitzvah in the seventh grade. How could I hook up with someone who is religious? I don't want things to get weird. I suddenly want to call Becky, but of course I forgot my cell phone. I'll call her later. She will be so excited for me. But I know that once I tell her, it's like telling the whole world. She has a big mouth.

The coffee is so good. I'm a little nervous that it will make me jumpy, but who cares? I already made an ass out of myself with the pot last night. I am sitting on the red couch and watching everyone at Starbucks. There are two ladies in the corner and they are in a deep conversation about something. It has be something about sex. There's a group of guys waiting in line and they are each a little edgy in their own way. One has dark hair and stud earrings and he's carrying a skateboard. He looks familiar. I think it might be a friend of Jack's. In fact, I know it is. His name is Mason Cleets and he is definitely friends with Jack. As I get up to throw out my cup and head for the door, Mason Cleets taps me on the shoulder.

"Hey," I say. I'm cool.

"Hey, Lacey, right?" he says. He's got a great smile and I can't believe I go a little hot when I look at him. It's not just Jack who has this effect on me.

"Where's Jack?" he says.

"I believe he is at church."

"Jack! I should have known, it's Sunday morning. Where else would he be?" he says.

"Oh, really? Jack is always at church on Sundays?" I ask.

"Yep. It's a little much, right?" he says with a grin.

"To each his own, I guess," I say, because, really, what else can I say?

Is it weird to be at church on Sundays? I don't know.

"Nice beach day," says Mason. "Are you going?"

"Um, I think I have other plans."

"Oh. Too bad. I would have invited you to come with me." Whoa.

"Really?" I ask. "I mean, really, that sounds nice. I guess I better get going. It was nice to see you, Mason."

"You, too. Lacey. Hope to see you around. I'm here on Sunday mornings." He's looking at me and I'm feeling really weird.

What is my problem? I was just flirting with Jack's friend. What's wrong with me? Or is it that I am sending out signals now that I am no longer a virgin? There's a whole universe out there with tons of hot guys, and I just may want to flirt with all of them. God help me. Maybe I need to start going to church. What would that be like?

When I get home from my coffee run, Mom's guest is gone, and I pretend that I know nothing about it.

"How was last night, Lacey?" Mom is buttering some toast at the kitchen table. She's wearing a black velour sweat suit and a pair of sneakers.

"We went to dinner."

"I'm going to take a bike ride today!" she announces.

"What's it been like five years since you were last on your bike?" I ask.

"Maybe! Who cares how long it's been?" Mom says, and shoots me a look like why do you always have to be a downer.

Over the years, Mom has tried at least a dozen times to get back in shape. It never goes well. Fitness magazines. Dumbbells. Protein shakes. She's tried it all.

"You better make sure you have air in your tires," I say, because I am such a bitch.

"Tell me about last night," she says.

"We went to Blue," I say.

Mom looks up at me.

"What?" I ask. She has a puzzled look on her face.

"I was there with my new friend," Mom says, blushing and giggling.

Oh my God. I could have run into her. That would have been a buzz kill.

"Your new friend?" I ask. "You made a new friend, Mom, how sweet," I say in a sarcastic tone.

Mom laughs.

"Oh, all right, I know it sounds weird. Yes, I have a new friend. He's the new gym teacher at my school."

"So that explains the bike ride," I say.

Mom is going to try and turn herself into a sports fanatic for this guy.

"Yes, well he is the gym teacher, for God's sakes. It would have been easier if he were the music teacher, or the art teacher. But, I guess then I would be singing show tunes or setting up an easel."

I pretend not to hear her.

"What did you eat at Blue? Wasn't it delicious? I had the chicken cordon bleu and James had the sea bass. We then split our meals, just like me and you do."

How cute. I am about to be sick. I nod.

Mom is gushing with details about her new friend. He's forty and he comes from Boston. He was married once ten years ago. Divorced. No kids. He's really smart and funny and he loves all sports. He doesn't mind that Mom doesn't care about sports. I am trying not to listen, not to show any signs of interest, because really, I don't give a crap. But before we go our separate ways for the day, I ask her a serious question.

"Why didn't we ever go to church?" I ask.

Mom says, "huh?"

"Church. How come we never go to church, not even on holidays?"

"Lacey, I don't know. I just don't feel the need to go to church, but Lacey, if you do, if you want to start going, I guess--."

"No, Mom, that's OK." I cut her off.

"I mean, I just never felt the need."

"Whatever," I say, and then I'm in my room with my door closed.

Mom gets me crazy. For the last six years, she was quiet and depressed and she never wanted to go anywhere. I begged her to take me places, do things with me. But she was too depressed. And now, her cloud is lifting. Well, that's great. But why didn't the cloud lift when I needed her to be with me? That just sucks for me.

Later I hang out with Becky and she wants all the details.

"So what's he like down there?" she asks.

"No, you did not ask that."

"Were you on top?" she goes on.

"Too much information for you, Beck."

I just don't feel like telling everything. So, I tell her the basics: Nice night. Romantic dinner at Blue. Some pot to relax. Beach. Hook up. End of story.

"I don't know why you are being so stingy with the details," she says.

"You are crazy," I say.

"So I have been told," she nods. Then she laughs an evil laugh.

"Come on, tell me something good," she says.

"Jack made me feel good," I say quietly.

"All right, now we are getting somewhere!" Becky exclaims, and then belches.

We are sitting outside on my porch, taking the sun in bikini tops and shorts. We're just shooting the breeze, when a black car pulls up in front of my house. A young guy walks out of the car and he's carrying a small package. As he approaches my door, he says, "Package for Lacey Bryce. Is that you?" he asks.

I nod and take the package.

The guy looks at me and smiles.

"Who are you?" I ask.

"Just the messenger. Have a nice day, ladies." The next thing I know he's back in his car. I look at Becky.

"What the hell is it?" says Becky.

"I don't know," I say.

"Make sure it's not ticking."

And I do. I put it to my ear, but I definitely don't hear a ticking.

"We're safe."

The box is wrapped in brown paper with a pink ribbon tied around it.

"I don't know if I should open it."

"What? Give me that. I'll open it. Are you friggin' nuts?" Becky says, and then she grabs the box out of my hands.

"I don't know if I should open it," she is teasing me.

"No, Becky," I shout. "Give it back," I say.

Becky decides to be really obnoxious, which is not unusual or difficult for her. She starts running away and making me chase her. Becky is a runner and she is like six feet tall. How is that a fair fight? As I am struggling to grab the box out of her hands, Becky is laughing at me and I am cursing her. I am about to start crying. Becky can really be frustrating. She's so bossy. Finally, she stops and hands me back the box.

"I don't want to open it just yet. Let's go get some lunch first," I say.

Here's what I'm thinking. If there is an embarrassing break up note, do I really want Becky around for that humiliation? I know she'll be sweet about it, but she will also pretty much write a press release about it and send it to the local paper. Becky doesn't mean to have such a big mouth. She can't help it, really. Her mom is the same way.

Becky is annoyed with me, but tough nuggies. We get dressed and get in her car, a dilapidated piece of silver junk that she lovingly calls, Carmine, and we drive to the Chicken Shack. We eat grilled chicken sandwiches and fries. Becky eats with her mouth opened. I tell her that this disgusts me, but she doesn't care. From time to time, she opens her mouth wide just to get me crazy.

"Keep your mouth shut, Beck, or I won't eat with you anymore."

"What is your problem about that box?" Becky asks.

"I don't know. I just don't want to know what's in it yet. Is that so wrong?"

Becky says I'm nuts, but she smiles, and I know we can get past it. As we're sitting at a booth, two friends from school, Bonnie and Whitney come by the table and join us. Bonnie is nice, but Whitney is so stuck up, I can hardly look at her.

"So, Lace, Becky here tells us you have a boyfriend?" says Whitney.

I glare at Becky. What a big mouth.

"Yep," I say.

"And he goes to Tollhouse. Excuse me!" she says. "Fancy, fancy."

"Yep," I say. "Why is this something that you need to know about?" I ask.

"Well, are you guys serious?" Whitney asks. "I'm just curious. I don't recall you having many boyfriends. Am I right?"

"Yep," I say.

I want to say, shut up you slut bitch. I haven't had many boyfriends because I wasn't attracted to scrawny pimply ugly little boys. I was waiting for a man. Why the hell should this bimbo care about what I do?

But that's it. She's not getting any details out of me. It's none of her business. I never liked Whitney. She always thought she was more popular than me, but you know what, she isn't. I have just as many friends as she does. I am way prettier than her and I have a personality. She just has a stick up her ass. Bonnie I can tolerate, but Whitney, I can't stand. She just rubs me the wrong way. Always has. So I turn it on her.

"So, Whitney, what are you doing this summer?"

Whitney loves talking about herself. "I'm taking a trip to California with my mom." "We are going to visit family. I've got a cool cousin in L.A. and we are going to party and go to bars. She is our age, but she has proof and she goes out like every night. She's actually a model."

"Cool. Maybe she can help you with a modeling career. I hear there's a real need for plus size models."

And just like that, I have the upper hand. Whitney is not fat, but she definitely has a few extra pounds on her.

She has made me stoop to a new low. I don't like saying things about anyone's weight. It's wrong, but that girl just gets me nuts and she brings out the mean in me.

Bonnie gives me a wink. She knows that Whitney is a jerk, too, but she can't do anything about it. Whitney is her only friend.

Whitney glares at me. She doesn't know what to say. I feel like punching her in the face. Instead, I smile.

After lunch, Whitney and Bonnie ask if we want to head to the beach. Becky really wants to go, but I refuse to. I say I've got homework, and a babysitting job at five. I am a big, fat liar, but I don't care. I just want to be in my room with that box.

I convince Becky to go to the beach with the girls. She drops me at my house. Carmine is humming loudly like she may be on her last ride. I give Beck a kiss on the cheek and promise to let her know what's in the box.

"Don't be afraid to open it, Lace. It's not going to be a bad thing."

At home, I check my Facebook and then I go on Jack's timeline. I come face to face with the picture of me and Jack smiling that he took last night. I admit, I look pretty and Jack looks so cute and irresistible. We look like the perfect couple. He's all smiles and I am like the adoring girlfriend. If I didn't know the people in the picture, I'd swear they were like prom king and queen. We're a couple, Facebook official and all, and if he wanted to put the brakes on us, it wouldn't say Jack Powers is in a relationship with Lacey Bryce.

I'm ready to open the box. Maybe it doesn't have anything to do with Jack. Who knows? Slowly, I open the ribbon. Just as I am about to open the box, there's a knock on my bedroom door.

"What?" I ask in my typical annoyed fashion. I am not happy about this interruption.

The door opens ajar. "Hey," says my mom.

"Hey," I say. "What do you need? I'm busy," I say.

"You don't look busy," says Mom.

Great. Let's get into an argument now about whether or not I'm busy.

"What did you need?" I repeat, refusing to make eye contact.

Mom is still in her black warm up suit.

"I'd like you to come say hello to my friend. He's in the kitchen."

I'm not really sure why I don't want to, but I know I don't want to.

"Please," she says.

"Why? I don't have to be his friend. You do. I'm happy in my room, Mom."

You never came out of your room for the longest time. I had friends over, and things happening, but you always had a headache or you weren't feeling up to it. And now, you'd like me to do this for you.

"I'd like you to come out and say hello. I'm not asking that much. I want you to come out and be polite and respectful, and then you can come back in here and close your door and get back to whatever the hell you were doing." She looks pretty pissed off at me and I just cannot handle another speech from her how we used to be so close and all. I realize I'm probably supposed to respond somehow. "Do you understand?"

I choose to say nothing. I just glare at her.

She just stands there, waiting for me to kiss her feet or something.

"Do you understand, Lacey?"

I don't answer. She shuts my door and leaves me sitting on the floor with the box on my lap. Crap. What the hell? I just sit there, unable to move, unable to think. And then, I know what I have to do. I stand up, brush my hair, put on a clean shirt and a bit of lip gloss. I look in the mirror and say out loud, "Hi, I'm Lacey. It's nice to meet you." I hold out my hand and pretend to shake. Then I stare at myself for a moment. "So, you and my mother are having sex, huh?"

I walk out the door and leave the box on my bed. I walk toward the kitchen. I am taken aback at the sight of this guy. He looks so young. He's wearing a big grin, as he talks to my mother about some team he played for in college. Mom is nodding and smiling and looking like she is happier than I have ever seen her. I'm actually wondering who this woman is.

"Lacey, dear," Mom says. "James, I'd like you to meet my Lacey. Lacey, this is my friend, James Breckinridge."

"Hello, Mr. Breckinridge. It's nice to meet you," I say in a robotic tone. I'm as polite as possible, but I don't smile.

"Call me, James, Lacey," he says.

"I think I feel more comfortable calling you Mr. Breckinridge, if that's all right. I'd like to stay and chat, really I would, but I have to study for a math quiz."

And before my mother can do anything about it, I am out of the room, away from her precious Mr. Breckinridge. I'm back to my box. I shut my door, sit on my bed, and begin opening the package. It feels so light, I almost think there isn't anything in it at all. That could be the joke. Inside the brown paper is a pretty blue box. In the box, is a pretty wad of pink lace. That's all. No card. No explanation. Just a wad of pink lace. It is pretty and delicate. I wrap it around my wrist. I can imagine it as a bracelet with small gems stones adhered to it. Maybe I will do that. I can go to the craft store and buy pretty stones.

My mother and Mr. Breckinridge go out to dinner and to a movie. I am happy to have the house to myself. I should be doing math, but instead, I am doing my toes. Then I am heating up a chicken pot pie and just watching the microwave like it's a TV screen, when the doorbell rings. My first thought is that it is Jack, and I hurry to the door. When I open it, I'm a little surprised to see the guy who first delivered the box to me.

"Are you Lacey Bryce?" he asks.

"You know I am," I am smiling.

"Right. Well, here's something else for you now. This here is a Starbucks decaf mocha coffee, and here's an envelope. Oh, and I'm supposed to make sure that you know that it's decaf."

I take the drink and the envelope.

"You have a fine night now," he says, and just like that, he is gone.

As I sip my yummy Starbucks, I open the envelope. It reads: This is where it all started.

Not sure what it means, but the whole thing makes me smile. The microwave beeps and my chicken pot pie is ready, but I am in the midst of a Jack attack.

I do not speak to him or text him that night, and even though it would be nice to say goodnight, I am feeling very happy. At school, the next day, I tell Becky what was in the box and then I tell her about the coffee and the note.

"Wow, that's so romantic," she says. "Who the hell knows what it means, but it is so romantic. I think I am going to start hanging out in Starbucks." she says. Then Becky belches. Long and hard.

"Really, Becky?" I say.

She is smiling from ear to ear.

"How could my best friend be so gross?"

"How could my best friend be such a wuss," Becky says.

"I am not a wuss. Not really. Why would you say that?"

"Because you don't know how great you are. You actually thought that there was a break up letter in that box, didn't you?" she asks.

I shrug my shoulders. " I don't know. Maybe. I'm not Jack. I don't know what he thinks."

"I'll tell you what he thinks. He thinks you're hot!" Becky shouts.

I don't get home from school until late on Monday because of Driver's Education. I roll in at about 5:30 and I expect to see my mom in the kitchen, but she isn't there. I'm starving, and annoyed, because I assume that she is out with her friend. I decide to text her.

Where are you?

Two seconds later, she responds.

Sorry I didn't get a chance to text you. It's Gramps.

Shit.

What's happening? Is he OK?

I am waiting for her to respond and it has been like a few minutes already, and somehow I get it in my head that Gramps has passed away, and she is wondering if she should tell me this news in a text.

I get a text, but it's not from Mom. It's from Jack.

Hey Babe. Miss you.

Really? Can a text actually make me weak in the knees?

Thanks for the coffee last nite.

Can I stop over tomorrow after school?

You bet. I delete that immediately.

Sure. Delete that.

I'll be around.

Homework?

Yes but something is up with Gramps. Waiting to hear.

Oh no. Don't worry.

OK

I call my mom's phone, but it goes to voicemail. I think I hate her. Why can't she call me and tell me what's going on? Is she with her new friend? What the hell?

My phone finally rings after I get out of the shower.

"Mom, what's going on? Why didn't you call me?"

"It's OK. I'm on my way home now. Gramps took a fall and he had to go the hospital."

"Oh my God, is he OK?" I say.

"He's all right, really. Just a sprained wrist. I just dropped him home. He's OK."

"Gramps. Why do these things keep happening to him?"

"He's getting old, and there's some memory loss. I don't know," she says.

"Yea, well it's scary," I say.

"Should I pick up a pizza?" Mom asks.

"Sounds good to me. I'm starving."

"I'll be home in 20," she says.

Twenty minutes later, I'm at the kitchen table with my AP global history text book. Bonnie is texting me about history homework. I have set the table for two and I can't wait to eat. When the door opens, I'm stunned. Mom is holding a pizza box in both hands. That's good. But who the hell is behind her? What's he doing here? Is she kidding? Mom sees me and flashes me a big grin.

"How's Gramps? How did he fall?" I ask.

"And hello to you, too," says Mom. Her eyes are pleading for me to behave.

"Hello, Mr. Breckinridge. Nice to see you again," I say, in my robotic tone.

James Breckinridge comes to life. He is so excited and he's smiling all over the place.

"I'm so glad you will join us for pizza, Lacey."

I almost choke. I will join them? Isn't it the other way around? What the hell? What is this guy doing here in our little kitchen? I don't know what else to do, so I grab another plate and another setting and take the pizza from Mom's hands and bring it to the table.

We all sit, and it's so damned ridiculous with Mom gushing and Mr. Breckinridge talking a mile a minute about his high school days. I try to focus the conversation on Gramps. But then the doorbell rings. Mr. Breckinridge is going to get it. Really? I follow behind him. It's my messenger boy.

"I'll get it," I say, pushing Breckinridge out of the way.

"It's my messenger!" I yelp.

This time he is carrying a piece of parchment paper rolled up with a hot pink ribbon.

"This is for the lady," he says. He hands it to me, and then he is gone.

Breckinridge looks at me with a big question mark. Mom comes in holding her slice of pizza in her hand.

"Who was that?" she asks.

"My messenger," I beam.

I untie the ribbon and open up the piece of parchment, and in the most beautiful handwriting it reads:

For Lacey

I'm no poet, that's for sure.

But I got you bad and there is no cure!

Thinking of you and your pretty face.

Seeing you makes my heart race.

Lacey, it's semi-formal time.

Be my date; it will be so sublime!

Wear pink and we will hold each other tight.

I promise you an awesome night!

Oh. My. God. I can't believe this. He did not say sublime! That is my favorite word (besides Jack). Sublime. Sublime. So that's what this was all about. His semi-formal. He's asking me to his semi-formal. I could hardly contain myself and I don't care who sees me. I am jumping up and down and laughing. I hand my mom the parchment paper for her to read. I don't care who knows.

The next thing I know, the bell rings. This time, it's Jack. It's really Jack. He's holding a tiny box. I am laughing and smiling and not bothering to introduce him to Mr. Breckinridge. I just look at him and smile and say, "Yes, yes, I'll go."

Jack is smiling, but of course, he is so well mannered that he takes the time to say hello to my mother and to introduce himself to Mr. Breckinridge, who tells Jack to call him James.

Then Jack hands me another box and tells me to open it.

Inside is the prettiest silver chain with a silver heart. It's perfect. I will never take it off.

Mom invites Jack for pizza and Jack is more than happy to sit at the table with the two of them and shoot the breeze over a slice of pizza. Mom is thoroughly engaged and Breckinridge is happy to have an attentive listener. When Jack finds out that Mr. Breckinridge is the gym teacher in Mom's school he is thrilled. Mom is smiling as she chews her crust. I want to be able to be light and easy with this little set up, but I just can't seem to breathe.

Mom is going on about how she is going to take me to Occasions tomorrow after school. It's a store in the mall that has more than a thousand gowns to choose from. Yes, I definitely want something pink, but I'm not sure which shade of pink, and yes, it would be great if I can get something in lace. But who knows?

Jack gives me a hug, and tells me he's got to go study for a test. Then Breckinridge says he has to prepare for tomorrow's classes. Mom walks her friend to his car, as I clean up the kitchen and get my clothes picked out for school the next day. I'm in bed later, just looking at my poem from Jack. I know it's sappy and silly, but it's really the best thing. Jack is definitely not a poet, but I love it, anyway. Mom knocks on my door. I don't answer. She opens the door, and pokes her head in. She has a big smile.

"I'm excited for you," she says in a low voice.

"Yep," I say, and my body goes all rigid.

"Lace, can I ask you something?" she says.

"What?"

"Why are you mad at me?" she asks in a small voice.

"What?" I say.

"You heard me. What did I do to you? Why have you been mad at me for like the last five years?"

I don't say anything. She continues to stand in the doorway, just waiting for some kind of explanation.

"I'm not the one who left. Your father left. I had no way to stop him. And just so you know, I begged him not to go, not to leave us, not to leave you," she offers.

"I don't care about that," I say.

"You don't?" she asks.

"I don't know." Maybe I do. Maybe I don't.

"Can't we be friends? There was a time when you really liked me."

"Why couldn't we be friends for the last five years? I tried, but you shut me out!" I yell.

"I just couldn't. I'm sorry. But I'm here now. Isn't that better than nothing?" she asks.

I just can't do this.

"I'm tired, Mom," I say.

She looks at me for a minute before closing the door. I shut the light and think about why I am so mad at her. I don't really know why. I do know that I don't want to go there. It hurts too much to think about things in the past. I just want to put all of it away and just think about Jack. So that's what I do. In my head, I try to imagine myself in a long pink dress.

Chapter Five

Just Like a Princess

I am overwhelmed. My mother is overwhelmed. There are so many dresses to choose from. Chiffon, silk, taffeta, lace, satin. Long, short. Dresses with rhinestones, dresses with cutout shapes to bare your belly. Dresses in the most beautiful shades of pink. I find about six that I want to try on. My mom has also found about six for me to try on. She has brought along a pair of heels so that we can get the full effect of the dress with the heels. I am wearing my silver necklace that Jack gave me last night. The saleslady is admiring my choices and tells me I have just the right skin tone for a pink dress. I smile. I may even smile at my mother. Slightly.

Dress after dress. Too much material. Not enough material. Too many rhinestones. Too plain. Too old. Too young. And then, there it is. A ballerina pink gown. The bodice is silk and tight fitting. A thin layer of lace flows over the silk. Wide shoulder straps gently hug my shoulders. The back of the dress is so dramatic. The material falls low and shows off my entire back. The front is simple, except for a ring of tiny rhinestones just below the bust line.

"It's to die for," says the saleslady.

Suddenly, everyone in the store is looking at me. My mother has tears in her eyes.

"This is it!" I say. "My dress."

"You think?" says the saleslady in a sarcastic tone. "It was made for you. Incredible."

Everyone nods around me.

It's decided that I will wear my hair up and I will have a French manicure with a pink tint to the polish. The shoes are going to be silver and very high.

When we get home, I make Becky come over. She sits on my bed, while I go off to the bathroom and pull on the dress, the heels, and toss my hair up in a bun. Then I shout to her to get ready. I ask her to introduce me as Jack Powers' date.

"Ladies and Germs, introducing the knock out babe named Lacey Bryce. Here she is all set to go to the formal with none other than gorgeous guy, Jack Powers. Everybody put your hands together for what is definitely going to be the hottest couple in town. Here we go. Miss Lacey Bryce is strutting down the red carpet."

"Holy shit, Lace! You are right out of Vogue Magazine. How did you find such a perfect dress, and Lacey, it's lace. That is so sweet. Turn around and let me see the back."

As I turn around, Becky screams. "Oh no you did not find a dress with the back that I have always wanted to wear. That is like the sexiest dress ever."

"So you like it?" I ask, laughing.

"Whatever gave you that idea?" Becky asks. "It's the best dress I've ever seen and you look awesome, girl. God, I wish I was going to this semi-formal to see everyone look at you. Doesn't Jack have any friends who would like to take me, your best friend, to the party?" Becky asks, and then she belches.

"You know I would have done that if I thought there was a possibility of a nice guy. Becky, I just don't know. I think you need a break. I don't want you getting hurt anymore."

"Whatever. Boys can't hurt me anymore." She purses her lips. "By the way, Lace, your boobs look boob-a-licious in that dress."

"They do?" I ask, feeling thrilled.

"They do. Trust me. Everyone is going to be looking at them," Becky says. "Enjoy it."

The next few days roll by quickly. I get a B- on a math test, which for me is like a small miracle. Jack and I have gone out twice since he's asked me to his semi-formal. One time we went to the beach with sandwiches. Then we hooked up under the stars. It was even better than the first time, because I wasn't scared. I knew exactly what to expect. Another time, we went out for pizza and Starbucks. We spent the whole time talking about the semi-formal, which is just a week away.

Jack will be hosting a pre-party at his house. Parents and kids are invited to that. We will be sharing a limo with two of his friends plus their dates. Jack is going to be wearing a tuxedo with a pink tie. After the party, which is being held at some ritzy boat club, we are going to go to the city to party.

On Thursday, the day of the semi-formal, my mother lets me skip school to get beautiful. I have a spray tan appointment at 11, a manicure and pedicure at 1, and hair and make-up at 4. By 5, I don't even recognize myself. Jack's party starts at 5:30, and once again, I am amazed at my mother. She is dressed in a short black cocktail dress and a pair of low heels. She looks really good, but I don't tell her that. She is all up in my face with compliments about how I look. But then, right before we head over to Jack's house, Mr. Breckinridge shows up in a dress shirt and tie. He's coming to the pre-party? Nobody asked me if I wanted him there. What the hell?

"What's Mr. Breckinridge doing here?" I ask, as we are at the front door.

"What do you mean? He's my date," Mom says.

"I didn't say that was OK," I say.

"Like it or lump it," Mom says.

She's so immature.

"Lump it," I mumble, and even though I look like a princess, I know that I am acting like an infant.

The party at Jack's house is in his backyard. Champagne is being served to the grown-ups, ginger ale for the kids, and elegant party foods are being passed around by two girls in black waitress uniforms. Jack's parents are milling around the grounds. Jack's younger sister, Adrian, who is 10, is wearing a party dress and hanging out with her own circle of friends. The weather is perfect. It's cool, dry, and sunny. When Jack sees me, he stops in his tracks and just stares at me. Then he walks over to me and embraces me in front of everyone.

"There are no words to describe how beautiful you are."

"Is that a good thing?" I ask.

"Totally. You look so pretty. The dress is awesome. And it's lace," he says. "Lace. It's perfect." "Yes. I never want to take it off," I smirk.

"Never?" Jack asks, with a sly expression.

"Well, maybe later. We'll see," I wink.

He kisses me. Slowly and softly. People are looking. Young people, as well as adults. My mother is looking. Everyone wants to see who Jack is with. It's me. Hello everyone. I am the lucky girl. Jack asks me to spin around so he can see the back of the dress. He nearly flips out.

"Whoa!" he exclaims. "Hot!"

"Speaking of hot, look at you!" I say, because that is the only word I can think of that describes the way he looks.

We are laughing and complimenting each other and I can feel so many eyes on me.

"Come on, let's introduce you to everyone."

Jack takes his arm and wraps it around me and walks me through the crowd, introducing me to everyone. There are a lot of stuck-up girls and I can feel some jealousy in the air. I just smile. Jack introduces me as his girlfriend and I want to melt. His parents come over to say hi, and they wrap me in their arms and welcome me. Adrian comes over to say hello, and gives me a kiss on the cheek. She is an awkward girl. She does not have Jack's good looks or his charm. She is shy and a little odd. Jack puts his hand on her shoulder and gives her a smile. He's so sweet.

Then come the photos. Pictures are being snapped from every angle. My mom comes along with Breckinridge and they begin chatting with Jack's parents. Jack's mother looks as if she's just walked out of a country club. She's very polite to my mother, setting her up with a drink and complimenting her on her dress. Breckinridge comes on strong. I can hear him from across the yard, going on about some football game. Whatever. The more I dislike him, the more other people around me seem to like him. Every once in a while, I catch my mom looking at me with a wide grin. I try to pretend I don't see her.

It's all good. The limos arrive and it's time for more pictures. We will be sharing our limo with Jack's friend, Noto, who is really sweet, and his high-maintenance girlfriend, who apparently is in her first year of college. She's kind of pretty, but has bad skin. I give her my warmest smile, but she seems to just look through me. There's also Jack's friend, Stark. He's a badass skateboarder and his girlfriend is really athletic. She says this is like her very first time in a dress. She's a little weird, and Stark is too, but I like them. When it's time to get going, the parents say goodbye to their kids with hugs and kisses. Jack's parents tell the parents not to leave the party. Breckinridge fills a plate and has a seat. I tell my mom not to expect me until morning, and she frowns, but we have been over this. Nobody is coming back until the morning. She has no choice, but to accept it. She hugs me and whispers to me that I look beautiful and that she is proud of me. I nod, and try to release myself from her grasp. Breckinridge is going on about some mishap at his prom, but nobody is listening. I wave goodbye to him.

In the limo, I am practically on Jack's lap. Each couple has a row of seating to themselves. The music is loud and techno. The liquor bottles come out and everyone begins to drink. Jack is on top of the world, but every once in a while, he comes back down to reality and gives me a tender smile. He says he loves the necklace that he bought me. Says it suits me.

The party is at a yacht club on the water. We are at a table with all of Jack's friends, including Mason Cleets. He is with a short-haired girl in a short black dress. He's definitely not having such a good time. I smile at him, and he winks. After we have some mingle time, the dinner is served. It is some kind of chicken and rice, but hardly anyone can eat it, because they are too busy on the dance floor, or too busy getting drunk. Jack insists that we each take at least five bites of the meal, so that we don't get sick from drinking on an empty stomach. He's so smart and responsible. After we eat, we are just staring at each other at the table thinking about how sublime it will be when we are all alone.

Jack tells me that he likes my mom's boyfriend.

I make a face like something smells bad.

"Why don't you like him?" he asks.

"I just don't know," I say, honestly.

"Well, your mom seems to really like him. She seems really happy with him."

"I guess."

"I'm just saying, Lacey. It would be a lot easier for you, if instead of fighting her on that, you joined her team."

"Let's change the subject," I say.

Jack brushes a hair out of my face and tells me that he loves my hair up.

"You can be so difficult," he teases.

I just roll my eyes and kiss his cheek.

Jack goes to the bathroom to smoke weed and drink from his flask. I can tell he's pretty lit. By 11, the party is over, and it's time to head for the city to a club that doesn't serve alcohol. The idea is that everyone will drink on the way to the city, so that by the time they get to the club, everyone will be out of their minds. Jack and I spend the whole ride into the city in a deep kiss. I wish we were alone, because I am feeling the love. As we reach our destiny, we all pile out of the limo and head for the club, which is called, Mind Game.

I know this. My feet are killing me. What I wouldn't give to be wearing a pair of Converse. The place is hopping. I hear a Maroon Five song, grab Jack's hand, and we hit the dance floor and have the time of our lives. In the bathroom later, I actually run into a girl who I knew in elementary school. She goes to Jack's school now. Her name is August Bantowsky. How could I forget that name? She is just as weird as she was when I knew her, but something about her is charming. She is a year older than me, in Jack's grade, and she came to the semi-formal with a bunch of girls. She is quick to tell me that she's not gay, she just couldn't find a guy she wanted to go with. When I tell her that I am with Jack Powers, her eyes almost pop out of her head.

"Huh," she says. "I never would have thought that."

"Why," I ask, a little hurt that she doesn't seem to think I am in Jack's league.

"I don't know. Jack's a nice guy, don't get me wrong. I just thought he would be going out with someone very Christian, you know?"

No, I don't know.

"I mean, are you very Christian?"

I shake my head.

"I didn't think so. He must really like you, then. I heard he only goes out with girls from his church."

August programs my cell number into her phone and says that we should hang out after school ends. Since she will be working at the library, and I will be working at my mom's camp as a counselor, we will both have some time to hang out. I think it's a good idea. What I do remember about August is that she's really smart and she has a sharp sense of humor that I enjoyed even as an elementary student.

"Sounds good, August. It was really nice running into you," I say, because it was.

Back in the limo, the driver doesn't seem to give a crap that we are all underage and drinking and smoking. I've had like two full joints and at least five shots of alcohol. People are talking about going back to the hotel. There is a party scheduled in one of the rooms, but Jack and I have other plans. A hotel room is not something that we can take for granted. When we get to the Days Inn, we say good night to everyone and Jack gets our room key and we head up to room 334. He's carrying a small gym bag that I don't remember seeing before. He explains that he asked my mom to pack a few things for me. I can't believe this. Only Jack can have that effect on a mom.

"Whoa, Jack. You think of everything! How do you do that?" I ask.

"It's a gift," he responds, and we both laugh.

Inside our room, Jack is drinking from his flask. He's also got a bottle of Southern Comfort packed in the bottom of his bag. If I drink any more, I will puke. But that doesn't stop Jack. He wants to take pictures of me in my dress. Jack loves taking pictures. He takes out an expensive camera from his bag. He takes a few head shots of me and then I tell him it's enough with the pictures. He says that I look so good in the dress, he doesn't want me out of it yet. So, we stand by the bed and kiss. I am too excited for words. His hands are up and down my bare back and it feels like I died and went to heaven. I'm definitely high, but I don't feel out of control. I just feel relaxed and alive. The room is spinning slightly, but I'm not fighting it. My words are coming out slightly muffled. But Jack is my anchor.

He is looking deep into my eyes, now. I can hardly take it. I want to scream, but I know better.

"All right," he says.

"What?" I ask.

"I'm ready for you to get out of the dress."

I could hardly breathe when the dress drops to the floor. I'm braless and just wearing a lace thong and heels. I've never done that for a guy before. I suddenly feel powerful and vulnerable at the same time. Jack looks at me and gulps.

"What is it, Jack?"

"It's you," he answers.

I belong to Jack. He takes me in his arms and we walk toward the bed.

Jack passes out a short while later.

"I'm starving. I could eat a horse. What do you say we get some breakfast? That will clear your head up."

"Good thinking, Jack," I say with a laugh.

As we walk to the pancake house, we are talking about the formal. After a stack of pancakes, an order of bacon, and a half of a bran muffin, I am about to bust. But my headache is gone and I feel great, just a little tired.

"What are you going to do for the rest of the day?" Jack asks.

"Well, I'm going to take a shower and then a nap. Then, I'm going to wake up and think about the night and relive it in my mind. I had a great time, Jack. It was awesome," I say.

"Thanks for coming with me."

I beam.

"It really was sublime, Jack. What a word! Only you can get away with that word."

"Sublime!" Jack says. "You are sublime."

Jack walks me home. I am so achy, even my lips are achy, which have been busy for the last few hours. Jack laughs and tells me he will be back at dinnertime to look at pictures from semi-formal and hang out.

"Jack," I say.

"Yeah, babe."

Did he just say that? I'm melting.

"Well, I was just wondering about something?"

"Yea," he asks. "What's that?"

"Church," I say. "What's that about for you?"

"What do you mean, what's it about?"

"Well, I just mean it seems like it's a big part of your life, but I don't know anything about it, and I'm curious."

Jack smiles.

"Well, church is church. It's a natural part of my family's life. I know it's not for everyone, and I don't try to enforce my feelings on anyone else. Church came into our lives at a really rough time. It helped us all cope."

"Oh."

It doesn't seem like Jack wants to talk anymore about this, so I just grab hold of his hand.

"One day," he says. "One day I'll tell you about it."

"OK," I say.

Jack stops walking and looks at me.

"You looked beautiful last night. And the lace, Lacey that was cool."

"Just so you know, Jack. I loved the way you asked me. I loved the messenger. Who was that guy?"

Jack laughs. "Frankie Lefcot. He goes to my school. He's a senior. Nice guy."

"It was so exciting. The lace set me off. Do you know I was afraid to open the box at first? I even put it to my ear to make sure it wasn't ticking. Can you believe that, Jack?"

We laugh.

"The piece of lace. I'm not sure what I am going to do with that, but something. Something really cool. I have to think. Maybe a bracelet or a necklace for Libby, my duck. "

When I get home, I am so tired, I feel like I can fall down. Mom wants details. I give her a brief synopsis of the night. I don't tell her about the part where Jack and I spent the night naked in each other's arms in a hotel room. I give her the G rated version. I tell her that Jack was the perfect gentleman. Then I tell my mom that I am about to hit the wall. She tells me to go to sleep and within minutes, I am gone. Dreaming of Jack. My Jack.

Chapter Six

Last Day of School

My last day of tenth grade is both good and bad. We just hang out and do nothing in all of my classes, but at lunchtime, I get called in to see Ms. Gregory, my guidance counselor.

Gregory is a freak. She makes a point to know each of her students, and she calls them in from time to time just for some "heavy" conversation. She cares about her students, but she goes overboard. When I come into her office, I am already thinking about how I am going to get out of her office.

"How are things, Lace?"

She wants intimate details. She wants to know if anyone in my house is doing drugs, or if someone is abusing me. This is the stuff she gets high off of.

"Great," I say with a big grin. "No complaints. It's all going good."

"So, what's up for the summer? You want to use the time wisely." she says.

"Got it covered. I'll be working at the camp where my mom works for the summer. I'm going to be a counselor for the five and six year olds," I say. "The day gets over at 2:45 and then I'll hit the beach."

"Stay out of the sun, Lace. You're very fair. Wear a hat, if you must go to the beach."

Yeah, like there's anyway I'm going to wear a hat. I nod.

"Do you think you might like to teach one day?" she asks, all serious.

"Nope. That's my mom's job. Not mine." I smile. I don't have any problems. Get out of my grill. Find someone else to do your guidance counselor dance on.

"Well, I hope you are planning to do something with your writing skills," she says.

"Yea," I nod. "That would be awesome. I like the idea of being a reporter, but I'm not sure yet," I say. I'm mad at myself that I let that spill.

"Well, you are a great writer, and that is what I wanted to talk to you about today!"

My brain is fried. I don't want to talk about anything serious on the last day of school. Just go away.

"Thanks," I say.

I am pinching the skin on my left arm with my right hand. I just want to get out of here, but I have to play Gregory's game, or God knows what she'll do me for. She is always volunteering her students for ridiculous stuff. I don't want to make her mad.

"I spoke with your teachers and with the exception of math, you've got straight As."

She spoke with my teachers? Why? What the hell?

"Straight As and a C in math," I say with a smile. "Math always gets me."

"We're starting up a writing program for eleventh and twelfth graders who show a lot of promise when it comes to writing. You have been recommended."

"Really," I say, with a big smile. Get me out of here. I just don't want to deal with this right now.

"It's going to be two classes each semester and you will get college credit for it. It's a lot of work, and the only requirement for getting in, other than having to be recommended by at least two teachers, which you were,   is that you spend some time over the summer writing a personal essay. You will submit the essay a week before the school year starts, and I will let you know then if you made it into the program."

"That sounds like a lot of work for summer vacation," I say, I mean, I am planning to spend a lot of time on Jack's baby blue beach blanket and that doesn't include me typing away on a computer.

"Don't be lazy. I hate lazy. You just have to write an essay. Five to seven pages in length, double spaced."

I stand up and make my way toward the door. "Great, I will think about it and get back to you!"

"Sit down, Bryce. Not finished yet."

Shit. Really? Is this how the year is going to end? I sit.

"All right. I'm up for it," I say. "What do I write about?" I ask, losing my patience.

"A personal essay. You have to write about some aspect of your life. Lacey," she says.

I'm thinking of writing an X-rated essay at this moment.

"We're excited to launch this program. There's a big budget. There will be guest writers, and book talks. I think it will really give you some direction about what you want to do in college."

I nod. "Direction sounds good." Let's wrap it up.

Gregory is so excited about this, she's about to explode. She's smiling and talking notes as she speaks.

"Your future is now. You know I always say that, right Lacey?"

"Yes, Ms.Gregory. I know," I say. The future sucks.

"That means you have to take it and run with it. Start thinking about who you want to be. Write about it. Keep a journal. Read as much as you can. Take it all in. Don't limit yourself to words. Take photos. Draw pictures. Think about where you want to be in five years. The future is now."

Buzz kill bitch, I think. "Sounds great," I say.

Ms. Gregory is always telling us that she understands the teenage mind. She knows that we'd rather be sleeping than working. She knows that we have all kinds or hormones running through our bodies tempting us to make bad choices. But she says we have to fight it. Fight it! She's crazy, but I accept the challenge of writing the essay. She actually makes me sign a form saying that I am committed to the class and will hand in a personal essay by the fifteenth of August. What a freak. She says that a copy of the form and a letter describing the program will be sent home. Oh, great. Let's get the other nut job on board. Mom will have an orgasm when she hears about this.

Then Gregory stands up. In her skinny black jeans and blue tank top, she almost looks like a student herself. She extends her arms and waits for me to hug her. I do. Awkward.

No time for small talk. Got to go, Gregory.

"Have a nice summer there!" I say.

As I leave her office, she is repeating her mantra: "The future is now, Lacey!"

I want to tell her, that right now, my mantra is Jack Powers, but I don't. I keep it to myself.

When the school day ends, everyone is all pumped up about a beach party tonight. Becky tells me that she really wants me to go with her, as she is leaving for Canada tomorrow and will not be back for three weeks. Jack was expecting me to hang out at his party, but under the circumstances, I decide I must go with Becky to the party. I figure, I will ask Jack if he wants to join us. If not, we can hook up after the party. When I tell Jack that I am going to the party with Becky, he seems pissed off.

"But I thought we were going to hang out. My buddy is having a kick ass party. I told you about it," he says on the phone.

"I know, Jack, but Becky is going away tomorrow for three weeks and I really want to get a chance to hang out with her. But you can come, it's totally fine. There's going to be tons of people there."

"Lacey, I really want to go to my friend's party. A couple of older guys who already graduated are in a band and they are going to be playing."

I know I have to be strong. I don't want to be the kind of girlfriend that puts her own life on hold to be with her guy.

"Why don't we meet up at a certain time? You can text me and we can meet somewhere by ten. How does that sound?" I say in a cheery voice, because, I really don't know how else to solve this one. As it is, Becky is calling Jack, Mr. Perfect in a sort of sarcastic tone. Becky really needs my help trying to score with Hoffman. I know he's a jerk, and she knows it too, but she has it really bad for him, and I promised I wouldn't judge her.

Jack agrees to text me around nine and we will take it from there. He may come to the party and hang out with me, or he may pick me up from the party and take me back to the party that his friend is having. Jack doesn't care if Becky comes with us or not. There. It's settled.

When I tell Becky that the deal is that at some point, we are going to meet up with Jack, she is less than thrilled, but she agrees to it, because she is so strung out about Hoffman.

She's standing in front of my mirror examining every part of her body. She's trying to pop a zit, and I tell her that's only going to make it stand out more. I put concealer on the zit.

"There," I say. "What zit?"

"Thanks. Hair down?" she asks.

"Yeah, but, brush it off your face."

"Nails green, pink, or blue?" she asks.

"Decisions, decisions," I say. "I don't think that detail is going to matter, do you?"

I know she's crazy with anticipation about this. She basically got a tip from someone that Hoffman is definitely going to be at the party tonight, and that apparently, he was asking a few people if they knew whether or not Becky was going. So, Becky is seeing this as her one last chance with Hoffman.

"I don't know what I am going to do if it doesn't work out with Hoff. We belong together. I know he was a jerk. I was a jerk, but I've never known anyone like him. He's so mysterious. He looks like Jesus. Doesn't he, Lace?"

I nod. "I guess. I have never seen Jesus."

"Shut up, Lace. You know what I mean. He has this mystique. People want to know him. That must have been like it was for Jesus Christ when he was walking around," Becky says.

"Becky, you're Jewish, and I don't know if you should be comparing the guy you love to Jesus. Something's odd about it," I say.

"Well, I am odd, in case you didn't know!" she says, and then she lets out a major burp.

"You? Odd?" I say. We both laugh.

Becky decides on blue nail polish, and I follow her lead. I am wearing a tight fitting black dress and a jean jacket over it, with flip flops. Nice and simple. My hair is down and full and wavy and Becky says it's really shiny.

It's a little uncomfortable when Breckinridge comes over to the house. Becky wants the 411 on the whole affair. She knows my mother for about ten years, and knows that in all that time, she has never had a man. Hell, in all that time, my mother has been like a hermit. Becky is all excited about this change. She senses my disgust, and tells me to knock it off.

"It's lonely out there. Kate Bryce needs a man. And he's cute. You better get over it, Missy."

"Thanks, Becky," I say. "Now shut up."

"I'm serious. Let her be happy. Don't you want that? You know, you're going to be away at college in two years. Your mom is a young woman with a lot of life left in her. Do you want her to be alone? Don't you want her to get a life?"

"Shut up, Becky," I say.

"No, I won't shut up. You're being such a baby about this. Get over yourself."

I am about to punch Becky in the throat. She can really push my buttons.

"What, you think only you deserve a boyfriend?" she says.

Now she's taking this too far, but that's Becky. It's what she does.

"You have nothing to complain about. It's the last day of school. You are going to have a painless job, and you will have lots of time to hang out with lover boy on the beach. I'm the one that is going to have the suckiest summer ever."

"Why do you say that?" I ask, relieved to get off the subject of my mother and her friend. "Canada is beautiful and you like your cousins and you like your parents, and when you get back, you will have a nice, easy time scooping ice cream at one of the busiest places by the beach. You stand to have an awesome summer. Especially if you end up hooking up with Hoffman tonight," I say.

"I love him," Becky says, and her expression is almost desperate.

She's so dramatic. But I can totally relate.

Becky takes one of my perfume bottles and sprays like the whole thing down her shirt and on her neck.

"Nice," I say. "Now everyone has to smell you."

Becky grimaces. I can tell she is really nervous about tonight. She's not being her chatty self. She's not singing in the car, burping, and flipping the stations around like a mad woman. She's just trying to keep herself chill and hoping for the best outcome.

It's a cold night, and the beach is windy. The party is packed, but we haven't seen Hoffman yet. People are drinking beers in blue plastic cups. Everyone is loud and psyched that school is out. It seems like everyone is in a good mood. Everyone except for Becky, who is just hoping to connect with her first love.

We hang out by the fire and talk to everyone. Bonnie and Whitney are there. Of course, Whitney has to ask me why my boyfriend isn't with me tonight. Why can't she just mind her own business? She just pisses me off. I glare at her. Bonnie gives me a wink, and whispers something to me, but I can't really hear what she says, but I sense that it's something like, don't sweat it, or ignore her. Something like that.

I smile because I know she's being nice.

"Jack is meeting us later," I say. I smile, because I can't wait to see him. I feel like I'm just doing my time here, and then I can relax and be with Jack. For now, I'm all about keeping Becky happy.

"Let's walk," she says. "Squeeze my hand if you see him."

Of course she means Hoffman. And he is pretty hard to miss. Even though it's dark here, Hoffman is really, really tall, and really loud. He has blond hair, which he always wears in a ponytail. He's also got the most unusual eyes. They are golden brown, but they have flecks of green in them. Hoffman is intense. He can be charming, but he can also be an asshole. I'm just hoping that if we do see him tonight, he plays the charmer, and not the asshole.

We walk around and on the way, we take a few hits off of a joint that someone passes to us. I inhale and wait for that familiar feeling to come over me. I just want to unwind and settle into my summer. It's going to be a really great summer. I can't wait to hang out with Jack.

Becky pinches my arm and I know that it has something to do with Hoffman. He's here. Like I said, he's hard to miss. He's wearing board shorts and a dark blue T-shirt. I can hear Becky breathing hard.

"Hold it together, girl," I say.

"Easy for you to say. Mr. Perfect's not here yet."

I laugh. I guess she's right about that. When I see Jack, I do breathe a lot harder and heavier.

Hoffman is standing behind us. He's talking to a few guys, and I don't think he's seen Becky yet.

"What's the plan?" I whisper to Becky. She always has a plan. Always has a strategy. She's a great problem solver.

Becky stands all of a sudden, and asks if anyone has a light. That gets the attention of Hoffman. He turns around and looks at Becky.

Their eyes lock. This can go either way.

Finally, Hoffman talks up. "Yes, I do. In my car. Come," says Hoffman.

And that is it. Becky walks over to him casually, like it's the most natural thing in the world. Forget about the fact that they haven't talked in like three months. Hoffman takes her hand in his and excuses himself. Becky is so under his spell, she doesn't ever look away from him. Next thing I know, they are out of sight.

I hope for Becky's sake, that this is a good move. If Hoffman sticks with his charming side, all will be right with the world. I glance at my phone and see that it's 8:35. Nice. I have a little more time to chill with my friends, and then I get my Jack.

I am looking all over for Becky and Hoffman, but there is no sign of them. I'm hoping that that is a good sign. A very good sign. I would text her, but I don't want to ruin her buzz, or disturb her. So, I just kind of forget about her, and make my way through the clusters of kids.

By 9:15, I'm wondering why Jack hasn't texted me yet. I keep think that he's going to just show up at the party, so I find myself looking for him. At 9:23, I text him: Hey, what's up? Let's get together.

I make sure that the volume on my phone is turned up so I don't miss his call. As it gets closer to ten, I am certain that Jack is just going to show up. I finally catch a glimpse of Becky and Hoffman, and it looks like Hoffman has his charming side on. Becky is holding his hand and laughing at his jokes. She eventually catches my eye, and comes over to me.

"Better than my wildest dreams," she whispers in my ear.

"Oh my God," I say. "I'm so happy for you."

"Where's lover boy?" she asks.

"I don't know. He was supposed to text, but maybe he is just coming here," I say, sounding casual, and not the slightest bit concerned. I take an extra big gulp of beer from Becky's cup.

"Mind if I go back to Hoffman?" she asks in a shy tone.

"I'd mind if you didn't," I say. "Good luck, Beck. Love you," I say.

"Right back at you," she says and she is gone.

I am left to wonder where Jack is. Why didn't he text me back? What is going on? Should I be concerned?

At eleven, I get a text that is almost unreadable:

Nvm too much to drink.

When I text back call me, he doesn't. Perfect Jack is too drunk to communicate with me. Now I definitely can't find Becky and Hoffman, and I am so going to need a ride home from someone. I hate being in that position. As it is, I'm one of the few people who don't drive yet. I'm combing the crowd in search of someone who hasn't had too much to drink, who I can ask to take me home. I am not coming up with much. I'm getting really angry right now. I don't know if the anger I am feeling is for Jack, or for me.

I am such an ass. I can't even believe that I have to call my mom at 11:45 and ask her for a ride home from the beach. She's all excited to hear my voice. She's just getting home with Breckinridge, but she would be happy to come and get me. She will see me in ten.

Ten minutes later, Breckinridge pulls up in his Toyota. My mom is in the front seat and they are smiling and waving to me as I cross the street and walk toward them. It's embarrassing to say the least. When she asks what happened to Becky, I just mumble something that makes absolutely no sense. When she asks about Jack, I just say he had his own party. "We don't always have to go out with each other, you know," I say.

When we get to the house, Mom and her friend ask if I want to stay up and talk. I would rather have a root canal. I tell them I'm too tired to keep my eyes open. I excuse myself and go to my room and hold my stuffed duck. Not a good night for me.

Chapter Seven

The Elements of a Relationship

Why didn't Jack call last night? Why didn't he text me? Was he trying to be spiteful, or did he really just drink too much? I am looking for answers to these and other questions. I am on my third cup of coffee when a text comes in. Jack? But it's not Jack. It's Becky. The text reads: I am going to marry Hoffman.

I laugh and write back: Does that mean I am your maid of honor?

Becky goes on: I am with Hoff now. We are heading for beach. Want 2 come?

I respond: No. Got a lot to do. Xo

I am happy for Becky. She is probably really bummed about having to leave for Canada this afternoon. But, at least she is back with the love of her life, or with the person she believes is the love of her life.

I am not calling Jack. He owes me an explanation. Here is what I know: Yesterday was the last day of school. Everyone was crazy excited about that. I had a party and Jack had a party. We agreed to meet up at some point in the night, but it never happened. Jack's text was probably a drunken message. I should not even think about it.

My mother gets the letter from Ms. Gregory. She is excited about it. She is suggesting that we brainstorm topics together for the personal essay that I have to write. I tell her to calm down. Then I suggest we take a trip to check in on Gramps.

Mom thinks this is a great idea, since Breckinridge is at the dentist and the bank. We make our way into the car and head for Gramps. When we get there, Gramps is sitting outside on his front porch. It's a sad scene. He's just sitting there by himself.

"Gramps," I call out to him and wave.

He sees me and smiles.

"Is that you, Rosey?"

Again it appears that Gramps has me confused with his wife.

"No, it's me, Lacey."

Gramps smiles.

"We were in the neighborhood, so we thought we'd come by and see how your arm is," Mom says.

Gramps is charming today. He is relaxed and feeling good. We sit with him on his porch. And, out of nowhere, Mom decides to invite him over to our house to meet her friend. Gramps accepts the invite. Mom gets all excited and goes into the house to pack a few things for Gramps, just in case he decides to sleep at our house. I'm thinking, how weird this is, but I am glad to have something else to think about besides my not-so perfect boyfriend, who still hasn't called or texted me.

Gramps tells me I am the love of his life and that he thinks I should be a movie star. I just laugh and put my arms around him. I let him wear my sunglasses.

"So where are we going, girls?" asks Gramps, as we get into the car.

"Dad, I just told you. We're going to my house. I want you to meet my friend, James," she says with a smile.

"Your friend, huh? Is it serious?" Gramps asks.

"Well, he's my good friend," says Mom.

"Ewww," I say.

"This ought to be fun," Gramps says.

Gramps laughs. He opens his window and lets the fresh air hit his face, as Mom drives away. I am in the backseat, checking my phone, making sure it still works, because, come on, what the hell is going on with Jack? What happened to him?

Gramps and I fall asleep in the car, so Mom decides to go to the supermarket while we are sleeping. When I wake up, we are almost home. I am groggy. As Mom turns in our driveway, I see Jack. He is standing in front of my house in shorts and a T-shirt with flip flops. He is carrying a Starbucks cup and a small shopping bag. He's looking at me with a serious face. I am not ready to be totally forgiving. Besides, I already have my favorite man in the car with me. Mom sees Jack and looks at me.

"Hmmm. What do we have here?" Mom asks.

"Jack." I breathe.

"Aren't you lucky?" she says. "If you want, invite him for dinner, Lace."

"I'll see," I say.

"Gramps, wake up, will you?" I say.

Jack walks to the driveway to greet us.

"Who do we have here?" says Gramps. "Is this young fella your friend, Kate?" he is asking my mom.

Gramps thinks that my mom is dating Jack.

"No, Dad, this is Lacey's friend, Jack," explains Mom.

"How do you do, sir?" Jack asks. He is helping Gramps out of the car. Gramps is looking at him and smiling.

"Are you a friend of my Lacey's?" he asks.

"I am," says Jack. "I am."

Gramps winks at me.

"Lacey, this is for you. Decaf iced coffee and here's something else." Jack hands the bag to me. In it, is a huge box of Good and Plenty. Good and Plenty. Jack remembered my favorite candy. He's got his arm around Gramps now, and he is walking him inside the house. He's just told my mom that he'll be right out to get the packages from the trunk. And, he's brought me coffee and my favorite candy of all time. He's back to being perfect.

When he comes back, I have a serious expression on my face. He comes up to me and kisses me on the lips. It's nice, but I feel like we need to talk before we go any further.

"What happened to you last night?" I ask.

"I got so wasted, Lace. I didn't mean to forget you. I really meant to meet up with you. Do you forgive me?" he asks.

"I do, but only because last night was crazy. Everyone was celebrating the last day of school."

"Tell me about it. My head is killing me," Jack says.

We kiss again, but this time, he's got his arms around me and it's nice.

"What do you think of Gramps?" I ask.

"He's a nice guy, Lace. He's funny and sharp. He already asked me what I want to study when I go to college."

"What do you want to study?" I ask.

"Communications. Computers. Engineering. I'm not exactly sure," he says.

"What about you?" he asks.

"I like to write," I say. "So something with writing."

"I've never read anything you wrote. Can I?" he asks.

"We'll see."

"Maybe we can go to the same college," he says. "Wouldn't that be fun, Lace?

I nod. Of course it would.

But can that really happen? And, anyway he is going into twelfth grade. I am going into eleventh grade. By the time I'm ready for college, will Jack be interested in me anymore? Only time will tell.

Jack brings in the packages and sets them down on the kitchen table. I start putting things away.

"Jack, do you want to stay for dinner?" I ask.

"Of course," he says.

I give him a big smile.

My mom is busy trying to get Gramps comfortable on the couch in the living room. As we are talking, Breckinridge comes into the house using the side door in the kitchen. He doesn't even knock. He's carrying a big box. He's got a huge smile on his face.

"Where is he?" he asks.

"Who?" I ask.

"Gramps, that's who. Where is he?"

"Hi James, how are you? It's nice to see you," says Jack, as he extends his hand to shake Breckinridge's hand.

"Great to see you, Jack. I hope you guys will join us for dinner."

Breckinridge goes out to the living room. Again. What the hell does he mean by that? It's like I am the guest and he lives here or something. Jack is totally into the idea of having dinner with Breckinridge and my mom. Jack picks up on my anger and puts his arm around me. We go on out to the living room to join Gramps and my mom.

Mom is excited to see Breckinridge. She takes his hand and leans toward her father. "This is my friend, Dad. This is James Breckinridge."

Gramps smiles and holds out his hand to shake Breckinridge's hand.

"That's a firm handshake you got there," says Gramps.

Breckinridge nods.

"You know what I always say about a firm handshake, right?" asks Gramps.

"No, what?" I ask.

"Nothing. Absolutely nothing," says Gramps.

I can't help but laugh, nobody else does. Oops.

We all sit in the living room, which is definitely the nicest part of our little house. The floors are shiny dark wood. In the center of the room is a fuzzy cream colored rug. There's a glass coffee table in the center of the rug. The couches and club chairs are black leather, and there are lots of animal print throw pillows. The walls are painted a very pale blue.

Jack is sitting in the leather club chair, and I am sitting on the arm of the chair. Jack is holding my hand. Gramps is on the couch, and Mom and Breckinridge are sitting on the couch opposite Gramps. Breckinridge is talking a mile a minute, and Jack is laughing and enjoying himself. My mother is beaming. This has always been her dream. It's like a real family. It's like a happy home. Gramps is acting friendly. He winks at me. It's decided that Jack and Breckinridge are going to make dinner for all of us. They go into the kitchen to go through the groceries to decide what they will make. My mom is tense as she walks through the house, trying to tidy things up.

The rest of the house is not so nice. Mom's room is basically just a room with green walls, a queen-sized bed, and a closet where all her clothes are. My room is at the back of the house and it's just pink walls, pink bedding, white dressers, and a desk with a computer. The kitchen is clean and comfortable, but it does not have granite countertops or anything fancy. It's just a basic house that hasn't seen much company or action in the eleven years that we've lived here.

Gramps likes it when I just talk about everyday stuff, so I do that. I tell him about how it feels great to finish another school year. I tell him about the writing program and the essay that I have to write. I even read him the letter from Gregory.

Gramps, because he knows me so well, is telling me not to leave the assignment for the last minute.

"Don't procrastinate, Lace. Get it done as soon as you can," he says.

"Thanks, Gramps," I say.

"You are going to procrastinate, aren't you?" he asks.

"Probably," I laugh.

I ask him what he would write about if he had to write a personal essay. He thinks for a minute. Just when I am about to think that he is going to fall asleep, he answers.

"Love. I would write about how much I loved my wife."

I think that is so beautiful. I know he loved Grandma Rosey very much. But I also know that they used to fight a lot. I can remember them arguing and calling each other names one minute, and then all happy the next minute.

"Would you write about one event, or would you just write about the relationship?" I ask.

Again, he is silent and doesn't seem to be responding to my question. After a few minutes, he starts talking.

"There was once a time when she said that she was not happy. We had been married for fourteen years. What do you mean not happy? It was nuts. She wanted to go away and think. We had two children. I thought she was crazy, but I let her go. It seemed wrong to make her stay against her will. For several days, I was alone to take care of your mom and her brother. I didn't hear from Rosey. They didn't have these crazy cellphones, and computers. I thought she was gone for good. I felt so lonely. Four days later, she came back into the house while we were having dinner. We were eating hot dogs and spaghetti, the two things I knew how to cook. I took one look at her, and I was so grateful that she had come back. She looked at me and told me that she had missed me and she was back for good. I grabbed her and kissed her. I set a plate for her and served her some food. We never talked about it again. I never asked her where she had been for those four days. I used to imagine where she could have gone, what she could have done. But I never asked her. It didn't seem right to ask her. But sometimes, when I am just thinking, I wonder where she went, and what happened to make her come back to me. That's what I would write about."

It's hard to imagine Gramps in a kitchen somewhere making hot dogs and spaghetti for two kids. It's a nice story. I wonder where my grandmother was during those days. Did she have a lover? I see that my mother is standing behind Gramps listening to the story. Does she know this story? Does she remember? Gramps is ready for a nap, so I let him close his eyes and kick back. I go in my room to put on something pretty. I settle on a solid blue T-shirt dress with a silver belt, and my cowboy boots. Then I check my phone and see that Becky has left me five text messages.

The first one reads: "Happy national sugar cookie day babe!" The next one reads: "Where the hell are you... Were you abducted by aliens?" That's one reason I love Becky so much. She can be the funniest person in the world, but she's tough shit when you need her to be. I don't bother to read the rest of the messages. I call her back, and she whispers to me that she is in love with Hoffman. This time it's the real deal. Hoffman has declared his love. Becky tells me that she is about to do something really crazy. She is letting her parents take her to the airport to go to Canada, but that she is going to leave her passport at home, so that she will not be allowed to get on the plane. That way, she will not have to leave Hoffman.

I wish Becky luck with her crazy plan, and she promises to text me to let me know if it worked. Then I tell her what's happening at my house and she can't believe it. Gramps, Breckinridge and Jack all at the house for dinner. "Take a chill pill, and make sure to get all the details down so I can get a good laugh," Becky says before she hangs up.

Mom has set the table and has put on a new floral dress. Mom is actually buying new clothes. This is serious. I can't seem to make eye contact with her. She is desperately trying to be friends, but there is something that keeps me on my guard with her. Why couldn't she be this way years ago when I needed her? She's all available and fun now, but where was she when I needed her? She was on the couch in the dark asking me to pass her her tea. When dinner is ready, we take our places at the table. I sit in between Jack and Gramps. This feels so weird. I am excited and I want to say out loud that I am between my two favorite guys. I don't dare say it, but I think it.

"Uh, what's the kid's name again?" Gramps points his fork in the direction of Jack, eyes squinting trying to remember his name.

"Jack, Dad." My mother's smile deflates. "His name is Jack. He is Lacey's boyfriend. Remember?"

A wave of awkward silence washes over the table.

"Of course I remember. Jack, I like you. I liked you from the first second I met you," Gramps says.

Jack is beaming. "And I like you! I liked you from the first second that Lacey talked about you."

Gramps nods to himself.

"So, has anyone seen The Hunger Games movie?" Breckinridge pipes up. Maybe he isn't so bad after all. He is getting my Mom out of my hair by spending time with her, and he is a nice guy, I guess. So what if he's sleeping with her? Gramps goes on about how he hasn't been to a movie in four years. Breckinridge tells him that he would love to take Gramps to the movies. They make plans to go in the next week or two. Gramps and Breckinridge at the movies.

Gramps says, "You got a deal,"

Breckinridge is smiling.

Jack and Breckinridge have made baked chicken and penne vodka. It's a delicious meal. Even Gramps likes it.

"This is a very special meal, and I would like to thank James and Jack for making it," Mom says.

She has this serious face on, and I am afraid I might throw up.

"I'd like to make a toast," says Breckinridge.

We all hold up our glasses. The adults have wine. Jack and I have sparkling water.

"To new beginnings," he says, winking at my mother, who is blushing.

Everyone clanks. It's a nice moment.

I squeeze Jack's thigh. Jack puts his arm around me and gives me a kiss on my cheek. I guess I could get used to this. It feels normal and fun. I like it.

After dinner, Breckinridge brings out a strawberry shortcake. That was what he was carrying in the box when he came into the kitchen. He says it's the best cake he's ever had. Sure enough, we all agree. Even Gramps. All in all, it's been a fun time.

Jack and I agree to do the dishes, while Mom and Breckinridge drive Gramps home. Gramps gives me a big hug and tells me to write my essay. Gramps says goodbye to Jack and tells him he hopes he sees him again soon. Mom tells me she won't be back for a few hours. I tell her that Jack and I are going out for a while. As soon as they leave, Jack and I are kissing.

"Go to your room, young lady," he says.

"Yes, sir," I say, laughing. Jack is right behind me and I am practically running.

Jack is in my room. He pulls me down on the bed. He sees Libby, my duck.

"It's weird to have you in my room," I say.

"Want me to leave?" he asks. He picks up Libby and holds her.

"No way."

Jack laughs.

"Thanks for the candy, Jack-o-lantern."

"I know you love Good and Plenty," he says.

"Do you want some Good and Plenty, Jack?" I shake the box.

Jack smirks. "No. I want you."

Jack is perfect. Everything about him. The way he talks, the way he looks at me. Me and Jack are in my bed, under the covers kissing and touching each other. I wish I could just shove this moment into an envelope, seal it, and keep it forever. It feels so good and right. Jack is on top of me and he's kissing my neck. His strong hands graze my back and he positions me even closer to him. I love how we fit together perfectly, as if he is a piece of a puzzle molded to me. Becky says most guys just do the deed, and then move on, but Jack is a cuddler. He likes to talk to me after we do it. About anything and everything. And, it's so easy to talk to him. There are no holes in the conversation or anything.

I glance at the clock and reality hits me like a ton of bricks. We really should be getting up and going out soon since my mom could stroll in any minute. Jack wants to head to the beach because some people he knows will be hanging out.

We dress quickly. I peek at Jack pulling on his clothes. He is looking at me in a way no one has before. It's as if he sees me for the girl I really am, and he likes what he sees.

"So, is this where you write?" he asks.

"Well, not exactly. Sometimes, I guess. I don't really have a place where I write. I have some journals that I like to write in, but I don't have to be in my room to do my writing."

"Can I read something of yours?" Jack asks.

"I'll let you. I promise I will. Just, not yet."

Jack looks a little disappointed.

"It's not you. It's me. I don't do well with feedback."

"I won't say anything. I just want to know you better."

I want to melt.

"You know me. All of me."

He kisses me and I know he's all right with that.

I check my phone and the popup of a text from Becky explains that her plan has worked. She has bought herself another week here before she will have to go to Canada for two weeks, not three weeks. Her parents had no idea that Becky forgot her passport on purpose. Becky played up the whole thing and cried real tears at the airport. Becky is too much. Love makes us do desperate things.

Before we leave my room, I make my bed. As I spread out my blankets, I think about how Jack and I did something very grown up in this bed that cannot be undone. Does that make me a grown up?

"Now you can always think about me when you go to bed," Jack says.

"You wish," I say. "Don't you know I have other things to do besides think about you?"

Jack just laughs.

"Like what?" he asks, pretending to be offended.

"Like math, baby. I have math to think about instead of you."

When we get to the beach, Jack takes out a joint and lights it up. When he hands it to me, I hesitate, but then he tells me that it will help me chill. So I take a few hits, but Jack smokes most of it. The party is not really a party at all. There are three guys and one other girl and they are hanging out on the rocks taking turns drinking from a bottle. Jack takes my hand and joins the group by taking the bottle. He drinks a long swig. Jack passes it to me, but I don't want it. Jack introduces me to the group, but I don't remember anyone's names. These guys are not familiar to me. They were not at the semi-formal. This is definitely a different crowd. Jack's got his arm around me, but I am not saying a word. It's like I am invisible. The girl in the group is a freak. She's totally wasted, and she's just chain smoking cigarettes and staring at one of the guys. Jack is really starting to hit the bottle and I am uncomfortable. I take out my phone. I text Becky.

Where r u?

Driving around with Hoff. Where r u?

At beach w J. Too much drinking.

OK Let me no if u need a ride.

Will do.

If Jack is not all right to drive, I will have Hoff pick us up and take us home. That was the topic of the first and second driver's ed class. Alcohol distorts your judgment. Period. So we hang out for another half hour. Jack is talking, but not to me. I've had it with this crowd. I want to leave. I ask Jack if I can talk to him. He nods and tells his friends he'll be right back. We walk a little before I speak.

"Jack, let's leave now."

"Why, it's fun, isn't it?" he asks.

"I'm sorry Jack. I just feel uncomfortable with this crowd."

"OK.. How about we go home in twenty minutes."

I nod. I guess I can do that.

Jack kisses me. He tastes like liquor, but I still want to kiss him. Why can't we go into the car and just hang out? Why does he want to hang out with these awful people? I don't get that.

I wouldn't mind going back to the car and just kissing, but Jack is determined to get back to the group. He pulls me on his lap, and I feel so awkward with these guys looking at me. Jack is definitely not understanding how I feel. Why can't he sense my discomfort?

I decide to give the whole situation another ten minutes. I listen to the guy with the braces tell the guy with the crew cut how he can kick his ass. Jack finds this very funny. Then the third guy, who happens to be good looking, starts humming a song. Jack finds this entertaining. It's bizarre. The girl is staring at her hands like she's never seen them before. I want to leave. Jack is hanging back, still drinking from the bottle. I take out my phone and text Becky.

SOS at Neptune Beach.

Five minutes later, she texts me back to tell me that she is on the way. I am starting to feel sick to my stomach. Another few minutes go by, and then I see Becky. She is walking toward the beach with Hoff.

"Becky," I say, like I am surprised to see her so Jack doesn't suspect. I rush toward her.

She gives me a hug. Hoff gives me a hello and smiles. He's got his charming side on. I whisper to Becky that I need her help with this one.

"Shit, Beck. Jack's drinking way too much and we need to leave this pathetic party." I whisper in Becky's ear.

Becky walks over to Jack and gives him a strange look. I can tell they don't like each other.

"Hey Becky," Jack says.

Becky nods and introduces Hoff to Jack.

"What's up?" says Hoff.

"Jack, time to go. Let's go for a ride in Hoff's car. Lacey wants to go," Becky says.

Jack looks confused for a minute. I don't know what will happen next. I think, maybe he might be mad that I called Becky. He just stands for a minute and thinks. Then he looks at me and I have a dumb expression on my face.

Then he laughs out loud and makes this loud, savage sound, like a bird call, or something. If anybody but Jack did it, I'd be like, what the hell, you freak of nature, but Jack did it, so it's kind of mysterious. Next thing I know, he's got his arm around me and we're walking to Hoff's car. Becky tells Jack that Hoff is her boyfriend.

Jack just nods. I climb into the backseat of Hoff's car. It's a big old Cadillac, and there's plenty of leg room. Jack rolls in right on top of me and holds me. Becky hops into the front seat with Hoff. Hoff starts the car. Becky puts on some Sugarland music. Becky and Hoff pause to take each other in. They start to kiss. Jack is drooling on my neck. He has too much of his weight on me. It hurts. I shift, and he tries to keep me in place.

"Jack, move over."

He shifts a bit, but I can see he's about to pass out. Nice. Really nice.

I'll say this. Hoff is a good driver. He stays within the speed limit. He makes sure everyone has their seatbelt on, and he doesn't want the music too loud. I like this about Hoff. Becky is singing and burping. Hoff is laughing. I am a bundle of nerves, and Jack is fast asleep. We get to my house first.

Hoff tells me not to worry. He will help Jack get home, even if he has to carry him to his door step. Becky gives me a trusting look. I know they will take care of him. Becky, of course knows where he lives, because we have done several drive bys.

"Thanks, so much, guys. Happy Summer!"

I make my way out of the car, careful not to wake my boyfriend. I shut the door.

Hoff pulls away slowly.

When I get home, I don't want to sleep in my bed. It creeps me out. Mom isn't home yet, but I am on the couch for the night.

I don't think Jack is so perfect.

Chapter Eight

Can This Really Be Happening?

The next morning, I decide to let Jack read some of my journal entries. It's a daring move, but maybe if he truly likes me on the outside, he'll like me on the inside. My journal entries are about me and my mom and the dad that I don't know. As I am gathering some of my writing, Jack calls me and asks me to lunch. His tone is somber. I'm not sure what to think. I put down the journals and sit on my bed and wait for Jack. Something is up.

Jack comes to the door looking tired and worn out. He kisses me on the cheek and asks what I feel like eating.

His serious tone is getting in the way of my appetite.

There is something really awful going on. I feel it, as I climb into his car and he starts the engine. It's amazing how a person can feel tension.

"Jack," I say. "You look so tired."

His eyes are blood shot.

"I didn't get any sleep," he says.

"Are you all right?" I ask. I feel scared.

"No, Lace. I'm not. I mean, I tried to reason with them, but they won't listen."

"Jack, I don't know what you mean."

He turns to face me. He moves closer and kisses me tenderly. It's a passionate kiss, but there is something very sad and desperate about it. I am thinking of all the possibilities. He's getting back together with an old girlfriend. He's sick. I don't know. But something about this kiss feels like goodbye.

I pull away. I look at him. Search his eyes for some answers.

He starts the car and pulls out of my driveway.

"Let's get some lunch. Maybe things won't seem so dismal after some lunch."

"You're scaring me," I say.

"I know, Lace. I'm scared, myself."

Jack is driving. I am freaking out. We pull into a diner in the next town. Jack parks and gets out of the car, and comes around to my side. He opens my door and says, "Come on, hon."

I look at him. Right then and there, I wrap my arms around him. I love him so much. He hugs me back for a long time. People are passing us and walking in and out of the restaurant, but we are locked in an embrace.

Slowly, I break away and wait for some explanation.

"I can't take another step. Tell me what's going on."

"It's about me," Jack says.

"OK," I say. "More."

"Do you think I have a drinking problem?"

"I don't know," I say. I'm being honest. "I was a little concerned because I didn't want you to drink and drive. I don't know. Are you mad at me? Did I get you in trouble?" I ask.

I can feel myself beginning to cry and I don't know if I can keep it together.

"No. You have nothing to do with it. They are sending me away. My parents."

"What?" My hands cover my face in horror. This can't be happening. They may as well cut my heart out. How could they do this to me? To us?

"Uncle Aiden's house in California."

"What?" I ask.

Jack nods. He runs his hands through his hair. It's a habit. Kind of like the way I bite my lower lip with my top teeth.

"When?" I ask.

"Soon. In a day or two."

"For how long?" I ask. I can't bear it.

"I don't know yet. It depends on me."

So that's it. He's leaving. I am losing him. It was too good to be true.

I feel dizzy like I might faint. I can't believe this.

"Are you all right?" Jack asks.

"You know the answer to that," I say.

"Let's get some lunch. We'll go inside and talk and make a plan. This isn't going to change us. Lacey, I don't want to lose you."

And then I see it. A tear is running down Jack's face.

He grabs my hand and we walk inside the diner. I try to put myself on cruise control. I pretend that I have no emotions. I am a blank space. I am Libby the stuffed duck. I don't feel. I am not alive.

Jack asks for a table for two. He asks if we can have a booth in the back, where there aren't too many people.

Jack slides in and I sit next to him. Not opposite him. I want to be close to him. I want him to rest his arm on my thigh. I want to lean on him.

"Let's share something."

I nod. I like that idea.

"Whatever you say. I like what you like," I say.

"I know," he says.

When the waiter comes, Jack orders a turkey club on white toast and two iced teas.

"I can't believe this, Jack. This was going to be my best summer, and now it's going to suck," I say.

"Please, don't make me feel worse. It's all my fault. If I didn't drink so much, they wouldn't have made me go away."

"Is there any way they would listen to reason? If you promise them that you won't drink, maybe they will let you stay," I say.

He shakes his head.

"You don't get it," he says. "We've been here before. The drinking screwed up everything. I tried not to do it, and they trusted me before, and it doesn't work."

"So this isn't a new problem?" I ask.

Jack shakes his head. "I don't know what it is. Why it is. I've been drinking since eighth grade. I don't know why I've let it get this far."

"How will going to California help?" I ask.

"Uncle Aiden is five years sober. He's a Marine. Total control freak. He's going to fix me." He spits out the fix me part in a sarcastic tone.

"You don't want to go, do you?" I ask.

"I don't want to leave you, Lacey. I wouldn't mind going, if it weren't for you. Why not go to California, you know? But you are here and I want to be with you. I tried telling them that, but they said that my drinking is out of control, and if they don't do something about it now, it may ruin my life. Then they said that if I really care for you as much as I say I do, then I owe it to you to get help."

"Do you believe that?"

The club sandwich comes to the table. It's enormous. Too large to pick up. It's too much work. I can't eat it. I won't.

Jack asks the waiter, who looks like a very nice man, for some extra mayo.

"Maybe," he says.

"Maybe it is something that I have to work on. I know that every time I get drunk, something bad happens. Last night, I got drunk, and I'm not even sure how it happened that Becky's tall friend drove me home."

"Hoff?" I say.

He nods. "I'm not sure what happened. I know you weren't happy hanging out with those guys and that I ruined the night after we had such a good time at your house and after I met Gramps. This morning, I couldn't remember where my car was."

"Did Hoff help you get in your house?" I ask.

"The guy's cool. He really is. He's so tall, too."

I laugh. Jack laughs.

"But when I got home, my parents were just waiting."

Jack stares at me.

"Forgive me, Lace. I'm so sorry. I ruined it for us." Jack gets angry and slams his fist on the table.

I lean in to him and kiss him. I can feel myself wanting to have a tremendous tantrum. This isn't fair. I can remember all the times I have said that to my mom. When other girls had dads who lived with them, I would cry to my mom, it's not fair. She would tell me that life isn't always fair. It was hard to accept that answer. I thought she was just being dismissive. I guess she was just being honest.

Jack is holding out the sandwich for me to bite. I take a tiny bite. It's good, but I can't eat it. Jack eats most of the sandwich, while I sip my iced tea.

The waiter comes over and drops the check. He smiles at me. Jack smiles back. He pulls out his wallet and throws down a wad of cash.

After lunch, we go to the beach. I am not wearing a bathing suit, but I do have a tank top on and a short skirt. Jack takes off his shirt. He's wearing khaki shorts and flip flops. We have the blue blanket and we lay down facing each other.

There are a few people on the beach, but I don't pay attention. I am too involved in Jack.

"Jack," I ask. "Does this have anything to do with church?"

Jack thinks. "I guess," he says. "See, remember when I told you that church came at a bad time in our lives?"

I nod.

Jack strokes my hair.

"My mother used to drink. It was really bad. Then somehow she found God. God helped her stop drinking. She thought going to church would help me stop drinking, but it didn't. God couldn't stop me."

"Uncle Aiden is going to help you stop?" I ask.

"I guess. I hope," he says.

"But, you know, Jack, the only person who can make you stop drinking is you."

Jack nods.

"What am I going to do without you, Lace? I finally found someone I really care about. Why is this happening to me?"

"To us," I mumble.

Jack pulls me close and kisses my neck. He whispers something, but I can't make it out.

"What did you say, Jack?" I ask.

Jack looks at me. His eyes are my eyes. I know what he said. I know what he said.

"I love you, Lace."

I sink deep inside Jack's neck. I don't want to face the world. I feel the hot sun on me, but I keep my eyes shut tight. I have to find a way to get through this. He will say goodbye, and I will say goodbye. We will kiss and hug and that will be that. I will go back to summer. I will start my job as counselor next week. I will see Becky and Gramps. I might even call that girl, August. I will get through this. I will. I will write my essay. I will practice driving. I will make a bracelet with my piece of lace. I will glue the lace to a piece of leather and make a cool cuff. I will hang out at Starbucks. I will swim. Swimming's good.

I stay with Jack throughout the day and into the night. We leave the beach and grab a slice of pizza for dinner. As the sun sets, we go back to the beach. It's there, that Jack and I have sex again for the last time. Once again, he tells me that he loves me, and I say it back to him.

When he drops me home, I can't get out of the car. I break down and cry. Jack cries, too. Just a little bit. I can't believe this situation. Jack helps me out of the car, and walks me to the door. I see Breckinridge's car in the driveway. I don't even care about that any more. I just care about Jack.

"I can't say goodbye," I say.

"No, of course not. I will call, email, text, and skype. I promise. And, Lace, I'll do what it takes to get back to you."

I'm full out sobbing now.

It's time to let go of his hand. It's time to walk inside the house. It's time to let him leave and go do what he has to do with Uncle Aiden.

It's the hardest thing, but I do it. I'm in the house and he's in his car and we are not Lacey and Jack. I am Lacey in New York, and he is Jack in California.

I've had pain in my life. A father who left. A broken rib. A sprained wrist. Nothing compares to this. I don't know if it is better to have loved and lost than never to have loved at all, because I feel so empty and bad and dead. I loved with all my heart and lost and now my heart is broken and I can't imagine ever feeling better.

Chapter Nine

Living With a Broken Heart

After Jack went away, I became a different person.

I don't smile. I don't talk. I just go about my business. My mom tries to help. She says that I would feel better if I could talk about it, but I can't even say Jack's name. Becky tries to get through to me as well. She comes over every few days with her nail polish kit. She burps all over the place, and talks about Hoff and Ryan Gosling. She says she misses the old me, but she understands that the new me is just the old me trying to cope with the pain and the misery.

After Jack went away, he sent me daily text messages and emails about how much he missed me and details about how well he was doing under Uncle Aiden's care. After seven days, the communication stopped. That's when I took off Jack's necklace and put it in the bottom of my jewelry box. It was like another dose of pure pain driving through my veins, traveling to my heart. But now, I don't expect to hear from him. I don't even check my phone.

Camp started last week. It's great. A bunch of five and six year olds are just what the doctor ordered for my broken heart. When I am with the kids, I don't have time to be depressed. I have to be on. I have to be funny. I have to be in control. The kids are really sweet and cute, and they say the most outrageous things. They don't have any filter. They just say whatever they think. It's amazing and really challenging. Little Constance has a full head of curls. She says the funniest things and she dreams about being a famous tap dancer. There's also Carly, who is the true definition of a cry baby. Whenever something doesn't go her way, which is basically the whole day, she cries. She's so cuddly and cute, though.

My favorite is Archer, who is a tiny little boy who talks with a lisp. Archer has this whole imaginary army of characters that he is always talking to. It's so adorable to watch. I wish I had an imagination like that.

One afternoon, I need some hydrogen peroxide to clean out a scrape that I got on my knee. I go into my mom's bathroom to get the stuff. Under the sink, I find an opened box with two pregnancy tests in it. One of the tests is missing. What can this mean? What is going on? I can't say anything to her. I wouldn't know what to say, anyway. I have been so absorbed in my own shit that I don't think I would even know it if my mom shaved her head. I've just been doing my thing and not paying attention to life outside myself and those little kids. But now, I've got to take stock. Is my mom pregnant? Are you kidding me? Can this be? I know James is practically here every night. When he's not here, he's at the camp. He's the counselor for the eleven-year-old-boys. They love him. They think he is the coolest person they have ever met. I hear the kids talking about counselor James all the time. I have to open my eyes and see what's going on.

Here's what I have observed: My mother and James are always together. He practically lives with us. The odd thing is that I don't really mind him. He seems to bring out the best in my mother. He makes her laugh.

Mom is definitely acting a little weird. And, she is more beautiful than she ever has been. She just has this new glow painted on her face, instead of the old blank expressions. She is trying to give me space. She knows my heart is broken. She has been leaving me little gifts every few days. Nothing big, just a few pairs of lace panties one day, a small leather journal the next, some vanilla perfume the next. She doesn't yell at me, or ask me to do anything. I can't remember the last time I washed my own clothes, or put the dishes away. Mom has been doing it all. It's like I'm on a leave of absence.

So I start slowly, but one day, I set the table for dinner. Another day, I wash all the towels. I know my mom appreciates the help, but she doesn't annoy me by saying anything about it. Gramps comes over for dinner one night and he just holds my hand. Mom has told him that Jack was sent away. He doesn't ask questions, or try to make it better. He just holds my hand, and I love him for that.

I have started writing the personal essay. I don't like anything I've written so far, but that's all right. One day, I will write something that will inspire me and that will be that. Until that day comes, I will keep attempting to write. It's all I can do.

I feel sluggish most days. I have no appetite and the smell of things that I used to love sicken me. I can't even think about having a cup of coffee. The smell makes me gag. I drink green tea. I don't eat much. I suck on ice chips. I eat yogurt at camp. I don't care about what I am wearing. It's a relief to be able to wear the camp T-shirt and blue shorts.

I am just waiting to feel better. I am waiting to want to watch a TV show. I am waiting to want to go to the movies with Becky. Waiting to want to put on eyeliner. Waiting to feel like myself. I don't believe how much a broken heart hurts. The pain is so big and vast. It's like a huge river that goes on and on without end.

I come home from camp one day, and I am sitting in the yard. I am exhausted from running around and chasing five year olds. Mom comes out with a bowl of cherries. She passes the bowl to me. I take a few cherries.

"They're sweet." I say.

Mom sits in the chair next to me. She doesn't say anything.

"Nice day," I say. "Not too hot."

"How are you?" Mom asks.

"Can we not?" I ask. "I can't talk about me, Mom."

"Can I talk about me?" she asks.

I don't understand. I look at her. She's smiling. Her hair is pulled back in a clip. Her face is sunburned. She is wearing a purple T-shirt and jean shorts. She actually looks better than I have ever seen her.

"You look really pretty." I say. It just comes out of my mouth.

Mom blushes.

"I have news."

This probably has something to do with the pregnancy test, but I am just not sure.

"What?" I ask.

"Well, it's big."

I look up at her. Just do it. Just tell me.

"You're going to be a big sister."

Silence. I am frozen in time. I don't feel anything. I can't seem to focus.

"Please say something."

But I can't. I have nothing in me.

"Uh. I don't know what to say." I am choked up.

She stands and puts her arms around me. It's kind of awkward, but I don't pull away. The human contact is healing. It is making me feel something other than the numbness I have had since Jack left. I am crying a little.

"My sweet baby, I am so sorry that you had to go through this. I love you so much. I have been wanting to tell you my news, every day for the last week, but I've been afraid about how you would react. I know you are in pain."

I just nod.

"You must think I'm awful. You probably think I'm too old."

I shake my head no. Mom is thirty-eight. By many standards, that's young. It's young enough to still have a baby.

"I love him, Lace."

I know she is talking about James and I nod.

He is good. I know it. I tried to fight it in the beginning because I felt threatened, replaced. But I know that he is a good match for her. I've never seen her happier.

"It wasn't an accident," she exclaims.

I don't have anything to say. I am listening to her. That is all I can do now. She moves back to her chair. I try my best to give her eye contact, and to show her the respect that she deserves.

"I've wanted another child since the day I gave birth to you. I love being a mom. I know we've had our bad days, really bad days, but I love you."

I nod. I know that. I know she loves me and she never did anything wrong. It's me that's been the pain in the ass. I judged her. I expected too much from her. For years, she was depressed and messed up, and I wanted her to take me places and do things with me and she just couldn't.

"It's like my second chance. And for James, his second chance. We're going to have a baby, Lace. A baby." She is jumping for joy now. "Little cries. Tiny booties. A new little person."

She's so excited and I just have to give her something.

"I know, Mom. It's great. Really it is."

She hugs me again. And for the first time, in like so long, I smile. I actually smile. Mom is overcome with relief.

"It's going to be a lot of fun, Mom."

And it will be. Babies make everything new again. Mom is out of her mind with glee. She unzips her shorts and shows me the bulge that is her baby. My sister or brother. James's son or daughter.

I see the bump.

"Thirteen weeks. Next week is the ultra sound. We're going to find out the sex of the baby. Can you believe it, Lace?"

"Wow," I say.

Of course, not everything is honky dory. Mom is afraid to tell Gramps the news. She doesn't know if and when they will get married. James definitely wants to tie the knot, but Mom's not so sure. But Mom can't imagine that Gramps will be happy if the baby is born out of wedlock.

The baby is due December third. That's amazing. That means that before the next Christmas, there will be a baby in the house. There will be a crib and a baby swing and a changing table. Suddenly, the house looks awfully small. And, it's like Mom can read my mind. She says we might get a bigger house in town. Or, we might be able to move into James's townhouse. It has three bedrooms in it.

I am dizzy with all the change in the air. I tell my mom that it's all good stuff, but I feel like I need to rest. She walks me to my room. She turns on my air conditioner. She says she'll wake me for dinner.

She leaves my room. I can't think straight. I close my eyes and try to picture Jack's face, but it has been erased from my memory. That is the worst part of it all. It's like he never existed. His Facebook has been deactivated. Maybe he was just a figment of my imagination. It's just too much for me to bear.

Chapter Ten

The End of Something

We are finger painting and the kids are crazy. They don't just want to put their fingerprints on the paper, they want to put their finger prints everywhere else. They make a huge mess, but I just look on with a smile. I am not feeling too well, and by the afternoon, I am really struggling. Mom is walking around the camp with her whistle. Her job is to keep all the campers happy. She sees me and waves. I wave to her, and she comes toward me. Ever since she came out with her news, she has been a different person. She is sunny and bright. Always smiling. It's me who has taken her dark and depressed side.

"You all right?"

"I'm definitely coming down with something," I tell her.

"You look pale," she says. "That's the problem with being around such little kids all the time. You always get what they have. It takes about six or seven years in the classroom before you build up a tolerance to their germs. When I first started teaching, I came down with everything," she says.

Mom feels my head and decides that I should go home and she will cover for me. She arranges a ride for me with a parent who has picked up her child early. The camp is only a five minute ride from my house.

As soon as I get to my house, I feel sick to my stomach. All of a sudden, something dawns on me. I march into my mother's bathroom. I find the box with the pregnancy test in it. I open up the wrapper and read the instructions. My heart is pounding. I pee on the stick. I end up peeing all over my fingers. I wait five minutes. During that time, I do not even think. I empty my mind. I imagine a can opener opening a can. The contents, which are my head, are being poured down the drain. Nothing left. I sit on the bathroom floor. I have no emotions.

After five minutes, I pick up the stick. I am face to face with a pink little plus sign. I am pregnant with Jack's baby. Jack, who is gone from my life. Jack, who I cannot picture anymore. I walk into my room. I shut the blinds and shut the lights. I take the stick to bed with me. I hold it in my hand. It's all I have left of Jack. Jack's baby. You have got to be kidding me.

I am sitting on my bed. Mom comes home and asks how I am. I tell her I'm okay. My phone rings. It's August. She wants to go out. Am I up for a ride? Why not? I've got nothing better to do, except plan for the arrival of Jack's baby, and really, I am just not up to that yet. I put my hair in a ponytail and I don't even bother to take off my camp shirt. Who cares what I look like? I'm pregnant.

August picks me up in a fire engine red corvette. Who would have expected that? August is the plain Jane type. She's got long, brown stringy hair, big bug eyes and pale skin. She could be pretty, but it just doesn't seem important to her. I like her a lot. She's real.

"Hey, what up?" she says.

"Hi, August. Nice car," I say.

"It's a good ride," she says. Then we both burst out laughing.

I get in the car and she smiles. She's wearing blue jeans and a blue top. Not exactly high fashion, but I should talk. I am in my camp outfit with white sneakers. Very attractive.

"Do you feel like getting something to eat?" she asks.

"I could eat," I say. Just not anything that I usually would want to eat.

"Hamburger Harry's?" she asks.

"Sure."

August likes classical music. It's definitely relaxing, but I feel like I'm driving in the car with Gramps.

"This music does not exactly fit the car, August," I say.

We both laugh. August nods.

"I know. I'm a weirdo."

"Whatever rocks your boat," I say.

I feel good now. Like I'm not even pregnant with Jack's baby. And a hamburger is starting to sound really good.

When we park at Hamburger Harry's, August is careful to park her car far away from a lot of traffic.

"Already smashed up this baby once."

"Oh my Gosh, really?" I ask.

"Yes, but it was a parking lot situation," she says.

As we walk to the restaurant, August spits out her gum. I stop to tie my shoe.

"So where is Jack?" she asks.

I swallow hard. I don't know. I want Jack.

"Jack had to go away," I say.

"Oh," she says. "Summer vacation? His parents have a lot of money, but I see the deli is still open this week," she says.

"No, he had to go to California to stay with his uncle for a while," I say.

August nods. She definitely picks up on the fact that there is some underlying story.

"Remember when I said that church comment to you?" she asks.

I nod.

"I didn't mean anything by it. I mean, just because I don't have any use for God, doesn't mean other people shouldn't. Jack is, for the most part, a very nice guy. He doesn't make fun of anybody," she says.

"Good to know," I say. "And, I didn't take offense when you said that. It was kind of weird to me that he went to church every Sunday."

"He's really smart and popular. But I guess you know that already. The thing that makes him different is that he treats everyone the same, you know?"

And I do know. Jack could never be a bully, like some popular guys.

We get inside the place and I am hungry. I order a big mouth burger. That's two burgers, cheddar cheese, pickles, and bacon on a sesame seed bun. August orders the plain burger. No surprise there.

She tells me about working in the library and how she likes it. She likes the quiet and the books. I guess I wouldn't mind that for a while, but I think I like noise too much.

"I'm really liking the kids that I work with. Five year olds are too much. They say whatever they are thinking. Even if it's an insult. Like they could look at you and say, 'You're fat. How did you get that way?' It's crazy."

"I'd hate that," she says.

"Yea, I guess it can get stale pretty soon," I say. "But it's nice to have all these little faces looking up at you and waiting for you to say something that's going to get them really excited.

The burgers come. Mine is like four times the size of hers.

"Look at this burger, My God," I say.

"What, are you eating for two?" August says.

Holy shit. Yes, I am as a matter of fact.

And just then, something comes over me and I decide to tell August my news.

"Actually, I am. I took a pregnancy test a few hours ago, and it turns out I am having Jack's baby."

I take a huge bite out of my burger. August is staring at me with her mouth opened.

"Oh my God, Lacey! What are you going to do? What did Jack say?" she asks.

"Jack doesn't know, and please don't tell anyone."

"You don't have to worry about that. I hardly talk to anyone, and I really wouldn't say anything. What can I do to help you? Do you want me to drive you some place? Planned Parenthood?" she asks.

"That's nice of you, August. I am still trying to get my hands around this. Jack doesn't know. I can't talk to him now," I say.

"What? You shouldn't have to take this on all by yourself. You should tell your mom. I remember your mom. She was pretty cool."

"Guess what?"

"What?" says August.

She still hasn't even touched her burger. I am in the midst of mine. It's definitely the best burger I have ever had."

"Mom's pregnant, too!" I say.

August looks horrified. She doesn't know what to say. Her bug eyes are popping out of her head. Suddenly, the whole thing is hilarious. I start laughing and then August starts laughing. The people at the next table are even laughing. For a minute, anyway.

"Say what?" she says.

"It's true. Mom is in a relationship now. She is going to have a baby. Hers was planned. Mine wasn't. Although, Jack's baby does sound appealing. Can you imagine how gorgeous he would be?" I say.

"Or she," August says.

I didn't even think that Jack's baby could be a girl. I just thought that Jack's baby would be a tiny version of Jack.

"You have to tell Jack," she says.

"Jack has a drinking problem and he's been sent away as a last ditch effort to clean up." I say. "Jack's gone from the equation. Please, August, don't tell anyone about Jack."

"I wouldn't. It's not my place and I wouldn't do that to you or Jack."

Now I put the burger down. My mood has changed. I don't want any more to eat. I have had all I can take.

"I'm here for you, Lacey. I know we haven't seen each other in like the last six or seven years, but if there's something I can do, please let me know."

I smile a tiny smile. I might take her up on that.

"Thanks, August. I appreciate that."

I excuse myself and go to the bathroom to have a good cry.

When I come back, August has paid the check and is waiting by the table.

"Let's go," she says. "Let's take a ride."

"Thanks for picking up the check," I say.

"No worries," she says.

"I'll pay next time," I say.

"Please, just let me be your friend," she says.

We go to the beach and sit on the rocks.

"You have to tell your mom," she says. "She'll understand. I know she will."

"Things aren't so cool with her. For the last six years, she's just been a royal pain in the ass, you know."

"Sure," says August. "I know how that goes."

I nod. I know I am not the only one who has issues with a parent.

"Listen, if you need money, I've got a few hundred that you could definitely borrow," August says.

"That's really nice, August. I don't know what I'm going to do. All I could think of is how much I miss Jack," I say.

There's not much else to say. It's nice just sitting there in silence and watching the waves roll in.

August drops me off at my house two hours later.

"I'm glad you told me," she says. "I'm here for you."

Then she high-fives me. It's a weird gesture, considering, I don't really ever high five people, but I know she means well. We agree to meet up later in the week. I tell her I will think about telling my mom. I watch her pull away in her sleek car.

I get into my bed. In the darkness, I think about how just when I thought my life couldn't get any worse, this happens. Jack? What now? What can I possibly do with this bit of news? Oh, and here's a fun factoid. I would have a baby and my baby would be Mom's grandbaby. Mom would be a mom and a grandmother. Mom's baby would be my baby's aunt.

I am not ready to be a Mom. I'm not ready to be seventeen. But how can I not keep every bit of Jack that I have? Maybe this is what I should write about. Imagine Gregory's face! To have Jack's baby or not? It's too awful. My thoughts get crazier and crazier until I eventually pass out.

I wake hours later with a shooting pain in my lower back. I think Mom must be home because I hear voices, but I cannot move. I feel like I might be dying. I am thinking that this is God's way of sparing me from any more pain. But, then, I think what about Jack's baby? If I die, what happens to Jack's baby? I have to save Jack's baby. I can't call out to Mom. I can just barely reach for my cell phone. I can text her. It takes forever to get the letters out.

Help me Mom.

I am drifting off. I am holding out my arms and waiting for Jack. I feel wet. I may be in the water. Something is off. My hand reaches down there and it's wet. I bring my hand up to my face and it smells like blood. I open my eyes and there's blood. I am bleeding. What does that mean? Do I have my period? It's a lot of blood. I am bleeding to death. I have to say goodbye to so many people. Tell Jack I love him.

The door bursts open. It's Mom and James. Mom is wearing a red nightgown and James is wearing sweat pants and a T-shirt.

Mom rushes toward me and puts her hands on my face.

"James!" she screams.

James comes closer.

"She's bleeding. My baby is bleeding," she cries.

I want to tell her that I have Jack's baby. I want to tell her that she's pretty. But I can't say anything.

"Should I call 911, or do you want me to take her to the emergency room? Just tell me, Kate. Tell me, what she needs." James is so nervous, he is practically crying.

They call an ambulance and my mother is weeping by my side. I don't know what she is thinking, but I am hoping that she sees the pregnancy stick in my hand. It is stuck in my hand.

"Are you pregnant, Lacey? Is that what's happening?" she asks.

She must see the stick that I left in the bed.

I try to nod. I think I am nodding, but I'm not sure.

I hear my mother gasp.

"You might lose the baby," she cries. "We're going to do everything we can. Just hold on, Lace. Do you want me to call Jack's parents?"

Somehow I manage to say a definite no.

They can't know about this. That's one thing I know for sure.

When I come to, I am in a hospital bed. My mother is by my side. I hurt.

"Mommy," I call.

She is kissing my face. She is telling me that everything is all right. I can't talk yet. I try, but my voice is so sore.

"Jack," I manage to say.

Mom looks at me.

"You were pregnant," she says. "You didn't tell me. You kept that secret. You poor baby."

"Jack," I say.

"What happened?" she asked.

"I don't know. I just figured it out. I was sick to my stomach all the time. I took the test."

"You are going to be fine," she says. Her eyes are swollen. She's been crying.

"Was pregnant? Not now?" I ask.

She shakes her head.

"The doctors did a pelvic exam and an ultra sound to determine that it was a miscarriage. Do you know what that is, Lacey?"

"Was pregnant?" I am confused.

Mom is talking to me like I am a baby, and I can see that she has been crying. She holds my hand.

"They are going to do a D and C on you now. It's just a little procedure."

I am going to have to have surgery? My eyes fill with tears. I'm really scared.

"You won't feel anything. The doctor promised me. They will dilate the cervix and gently remove any tissue that is left in the uterus," she explains, her voice sounds robotic, and I can tell that she is just repeating what they told her.

"No baby?" I ask.

Mom shakes her head and begins to cry. "No. The fertilized egg in the uterus did not develop normally. That's what they said, Lace. It wasn't meant to be," she says. "It was never going to be a baby. It wasn't right."

"I keep losing things, Mommy," I say, and the tears come.

A nurse comes in to start a drip in my arm. Another one comes in and gives me a needle in my arm. I begin to feel woozy. I welcome the feeling. I don't want to think anymore. Jack is gone from me for good. I can hear my mom saying things to reassure me. "I'll be right here. Just relax, honey. It's going to be all right. We will be all right. Then I'll take you home and make you better."

And it's just then that I wish Mom could read me a story. Are You My Mother? Or any story. Just read it to me.

I remember them wheeling me back. I finally don't have any more pain in my back. The pain was the baby. It's out and now I am just sore. I see Mom's face. She is trying hard to smile and to be strong.

"It's all over now. You just need to rest. You are going to stay overnight and tomorrow I'll take you home, Lacey. You are fine now. You may be sore, but the pain that you were in should be gone. The doctor said you might bleed a bit, but it should stop in an hour or two. Do you understand, Lacey?"

I nod. I understand. I understand everything. I shut my eyes because I am so tired.

"Good night, Mommy," I say.

"Good night, Baby," she says. "And listen to me, you can tell me anything. Anything, do you hear?" she asks.

I think I respond. I wink or nod or something.

And to myself, I say goodnight to Jack and to his baby, who is no more. But, if what the doctor said is true, that baby never would have been. I guess I should feel lucky. No teenage pregnancy for me. It's all done and over. Just like that. Jack one minute. No Jack the next minute.

Chapter Eleven

The Beginning of Something

I love Becky because she always knows what to say. Mom has called her and has told her everything we went through and how I was pregnant and how I got sick and had a miscarriage and how I needed surgery. The doctors said everything is good to go. I'm going to be fine. Mom told her that I've been resting for the last few days, and now she thinks it's time for me to see my best friend. Becky comes over about twenty minutes after Mom's call. She's got flowers in one hand from the grocery store. In the other hand, she's got a bag from the Chinese take-out place. It's a bag with two egg rolls and two spring rolls. She knows what I like.

When she comes into my room, I am so happy to see her, I just want to laugh and cry at the same time. She puts the flowers down and the bag of Chinese and she gets right into bed with me. My mom is in the room, and she makes her way to leave, but I don't want her to leave just yet. I want her to stay and be a part of this. My mom has gone through so much these last few days.

"Mom, stay," I say. "Don't go."

Mom is so touched by that, she moves in and starts massaging my feet.

"What the hell is going on?" Becky asks, then she burps about seven times.

My mom smiles at her. "Ahhh, Becky. So refreshing!"

"I'm all right, Beck. I'm going to be okay."

"I know that. I'm just happy that you know it. I missed you so much."

The three of us are silent for a bit. Words just don't seem to matter.

How was Canada?" I ask.

"It sucked, really. I mean it was just boring and the people there they just don't get me."

Me and mom laugh. Becky is hilarious with her long brown hair, her freckles, and her burping habit. Then she pauses and for a second, she looks like a little girl.

"Do you want to talk about it, Lacey?"

"Not really," I say. "I've talked about it a lot with Mom."

We are all quiet again in the bed.

"That is so great, Lace. Kate. So happy you guys are talking. What's it been, like six years?"

Mom and I laugh again. Becky.

"So, when do you find out the sex of the baby?" she asks.

"Tomorrow," my mom answers. "I think it's a boy. It feels different than when I was pregnant with Lace."

"Oh, Lace, is it wrong to talk about babies and pregnancy? Please forgive me. You know how I always mess things up that way. I don't want you to feel worse."

"No," I say. "It's not wrong at all. It's what I am looking forward to most. I am so excited to be a big sister," I say with a smile.

Mom looks overjoyed.

"It's been a while since I've seen you smile, kid. It's a beautiful thing," Becky says.

Becky opens up the bag and takes out the container. She holds a spring roll to my lips and says, "Dig in."

And I do. It's so good.

Becky passes the spring roll to my mom and she takes a big bite. Then Becky takes a bite.

"I want to know names, Kate. What are you thinking?" Becky asks.

"Well," says my mom. "If it's a boy, we like Tyler or Evan. If it's a girl, we like Violet or Daisy."

"Love those names! " Becky says. "So much!"

"I like them, too. I love Evan. I really love Daisy," I say, and I do.

"When can I take this beautiful girl out?" Becky asks my mom.

"In a few days she will be good as new."

"Excellent," says Becky. "I want to take you to dinner and a movie first. Then, Hoff and I want you to meet someone."

"I don't know, Beck. I'm still not ready to go out there and you know."

Becky nods. "Ok, we'll wait a week on that one."

I laugh. My mom laughs.

"Now give me some egg roll, Becky," I say.

And she does. It's so delicious.

On August 15th, I submit a personal essay to Gregory. I wrote it 15 times before I produced something that I could share with a reader. In the end, I decided to write about how I felt about becoming a big sister to the unborn child that my mom is carrying. I wrote about how, in most cases, the big sister is very young, usually not more than four or five, when she finds out that there is going to be a new baby in the house. My situation would definitely not be the norm. I would be seventeen years older than my sister. I would not be able to share a childhood with this person, but I could definitely share my insight and my experience. And then, I wrote about what I might expect to learn from this baby, this child. I wrote that I am hoping to be reminded of so many life lessons, and that keeping track of the many benchmarks, all the firsts, will help me remember and treasure my own childhood.

When I got accepted into the writing program, I decided that no matter what I do with my life, whether I become a mortician, an electrician, or a circus clown, I will always be a writer.

A week before the school year begins, my mom married James Breckinridge, who happens to be a really nice guy. The wedding was a simple ceremony in the backyard. Gramps walked Mom down the aisle. I was the maid of honor and I held a beautiful bouquet of daisies. After the ceremony, we all went to dinner at a beautiful restaurant on the water. Becky and Hoff were invited. August came to the restaurant. She, by the way, is a really good friend. I don't love the way she insists on high-fiving me all the time, but I have to accept people for who they are.

A week after school started, I drove myself, yes, drove myself to Starbucks for a cup of decaf coffee. I sat at a table in the corner. I listened to my iPod and sipped my coffee, and watched the people flutter in and out of the place. I felt a rush of adrenaline when I saw him walk in. He looked like he had grown a few inches and his hair was darker than I remembered.

"Lacey?" he said.

"Hey, how are you?" I asked.

We started a conversation, and I invited him to sit with me. Turns out, Mason Cleets is also a writer. We have become good friends. He's someone I can really talk to. Mason has made it clear that he would like to go out on a real date. I am taking it into consideration, but I don't know. I don't want to ruin a good friendship. We meet once a week for a cup of Joe and a chat. I am in no hurry to date, so for now, this is a great alternative. Mason says he's not going anywhere.

Mom's doing really well with her pregnancy. She hasn't gained too much weight. Her feet aren't swollen. She's tired at the end of the day, but she is also feeling more energetic now that she is far into her second trimester. I don't feel any of the anger that I used to feel toward her. I just love her. She is so happy to have me back.

It turns out that James is really handy around the house. Instead of moving to his place, or to a bigger place, James sold his townhouse. With the money he got for it, he is building a sweet addition in our house. In the back end of the house, James has built the cutest nursery. It's so adorable. The walls are pink and yellow and there is a border of daisies at the top of the walls. Gramps bought a beautiful rocking chair for the room. It's so pretty. Mom found a pillow with a big daisy on it. The pillow rests on the chair. The room is just waiting for the baby. Sometimes I just sit in the room and think about what could have been.

James has also built a family room with couches and a fireplace. The whole house has a different feel to it now. Mom tossed out her old stuff and bought new things. She says it's like getting a face lift. It's very exciting. There is a feeling like something great is coming and we all can't wait to meet her. It's a feeling of promise.

Gramps continues to be forgetful, but he is in a good mood these days. That's because he has a new love named Rosey-O. She has four legs and a tail, and she is the apple of Gramps' eye. Gramps is truly excited about baby Daisy, but he tells me that no matter what, I will always be his great love.

In the fall, I cut my hair to my shoulders and get red highlights. It's a new look, and it makes me feel fresh and confident. The day after Thanksgiving, I make a Starbucks run before Becky and I head out to the mall to do some serious Christmas shopping. I am dressed in Uggs, black jeans and a pale pink jersey with a dark long sweater. I am waiting in line, trying to decide between a hot chocolate and a decaf coffee, when I feel a tap on my shoulder. I turn around and there he is. Jack. He is thinner than I remember, and his hair is cut very short. He wears a grey sweater, dark blue jeans and work boots. I feel a choking sensation in my throat.

"Lacey," he says, with a glint in his eyes and the softest smile.

"Jack. I can't believe it," I say. He's standing right here. He's right here in my grasp.

"It feels like forever, right?" he asks.

I nod. Forever is right.

"How are you?" I ask

"I'm all right. Just in for the holiday," he says. "Happy Thanksgiving!"

"Thanks," I say. "Gobble, gobble."

I can't seem to find words.

The barista asks what I'd like. Jack takes over, and asks what I'm having.

"Hot chocolate," I whisper.

"Two hot chocolates," says Jack. "With whipped cream. Grande."

The drinks are up in no time, and Jack pays for them, and I thank him.

"It's so good to see you, Jack," I say.

"So good, Lace. You look awesome."

We are standing inches from each other. I resist the temptation to hold him close and run away with him. My Jack.

"I," Jack stammers. "I want to say how sorry I am. I couldn't stay in touch, you know. I had to stick to the program."

I put my index finger over my lips.

"You don't have to say sorry." I remember a line from Love Story: Love means never having to say you're sorry.

"There's so much I want to tell you," he says.

I nod. "I know. So much has happened."

"Listen, I'll be home at Christmas for good. I've done what I set out to do. It wasn't easy, but I'm set. I'm good," he says.

"That's great news, Jack," I say, and I smile.

"You look so pretty. So grown up," he says.

"That happens, doesn't it?" I say.

"Do you think we can get together?" he asks.

I really want to. But I'm so scared. I went through so much pain. It was awful. The days and nights of emptiness. Grieving. Losing the baby. You don't know any of this.

"We can catch up and have dinner," Jack goes on. He really wants this.

"I'm not sure." I say, my face twists in weird ways.

"I understand," he says.

"I want to, but," I say.

"Well, I'm back for good at Christmas. That's in just one month. I'll call you. Maybe we can hang out. How does that sound, Lace?" he asks.

I can tell from his eyes that he is not Perfect Jack anymore. And maybe that makes him even more perfect. For me.

"I think that sounds like a plan, Jack," I say.

He smiles first. Then I smile. Jack notices the keys in my hand.

"Lacey, are you driving?" he asks.

"Yep," I say, beaming.

Jack laughs. It sounds so good, like medicine.

"Really great to see you, Jack," I say. I lean in for a quick kiss on the cheek. I turn around slowly, and walk out of Starbucks, and head to my car.

Jack attack.

The end.

ABOUT THE AUTHOR

Jamie McGillian is the author of *The Kids' Money Book* (Sterling), and *The Busy Mom's Book of Preschool Activities* (Sterling). This is her first young adult novel. She was an editor for several years at Sesame Workshop. McGillian writes curriculum and children's books and lives with her husband, two daughters, and pug by the Hudson River in New York.